Captain BRITAIN ™

BY

ALAN DAVIS

AND

JAMIE DELANO

DIPPED IN MAGIC,
CLOTHED IN SCIENCE ...

MARVEL®

Published by Marvel Comics Ltd., a New World Pictures Company, Arundel House, 13/15 Arundel Street, London WC2.

INTRODUCTION

Once upon a time, O best beloved – and a very, very long time ago it was, way back in the happy, halcyon, innocent days before Thatcher and Reagan when some of us were a lot younger than we care now to admit – Marvel Comics, in its infinite corporate wisdom, came up with the notion of producing an original series of comics for the UK market. Instead of publishing reprints of already extant American material, or distributing the current run of US titles, we'd do a series about Britons, set in Britain and published in Britain. To compete with a hefty collection of weekly British comic magazines, we'd create a – hopefully – top-drawer hero, in the tradition of Captain America, who would spearhead Marvel's drive for international dominance. Because a flagship figure was wanted for this flagship book, the character was christened **CAPTAIN BRITAIN**. Thing was, in those Dark Ages – before anyone Over Here knew quite what was what Over There – nobody was sure if there were writers and artists who could handle Marvel-type characters and Marvel-type stories, especially since the creative editing on the book would be handled in New York (no faxing back then, and no international Federal Express either, which meant the deadline pressures would be horrendous). So, I was tapped to create the character and write the series (hey, I'm a Londoner by birth, they figured that must count for something, right?) and Herb Trimpe – who at the time was living in Cornwall (and who was, and is, not only an ace at meeting deadlines, but also one of the best story-tellers in the business, and an absolute prince to work with) – was chosen to pencil it.

I lasted ten issues, Herb not much longer, and my favourite memory of the whole experience was a review in the *Financial Times* – one I've treasured ever since – which described the premiere issue as a "farrago of illiterate SF nonsense."

That was then, this is now and, as the saying goes, things have changed.

Homegrown, world-class British talent – heirs to the legacy of Frank Hampson, Frank Bellamy, Jim Holdaway, Sidney Jordan, Peter O'Donnell (to name but a few of the artists and writers whose work I remember – and treasure – from my youth) – had come on the scene with a vengeance, their dynamic, exciting, occasionally ground-breaking, work building a passionate following Over There and attracting the attention of the US publishers. John Bolton, Brian Bolland, Pat Mills, Joe Colquhoun, Mick McMahon, Kevin O'Neill, Dave Gibbons, Ian Gibson, Garry Leach, David Lloyd, Steve Dillon, Paul Neary, Alan Moore – to name an enthusiastic handful – in series like CHARLEY'S WAR, JUDGE DREDD, NEMESIS THE WARLOCK, V FOR VENDETTA, and LASER ERASER AND PRESS-BUTTON.

Oh yes, and, among that cavalcade, Alan Davis and **CAPTAIN BRITAIN.**

Over the years since his debut, the poor Captain more or less floundered. Costume changes, role changes – super hero action adventure segueing sideways into outright fantasy and science fiction – but nothing had ever seemed to jell. Then, in the early eighties, Marvel UK editor Paul Neary (multi-talented rogue that he is) banged heads with Alan Davis and set about trying to define and then fulfil the potential they felt existed within the character. From that new beginning, and later with the teaming of Alan Davis and writer Alan Moore, the series took off like nobody's business – and hasn't looked back since.

What you have here is a compendium of the final seventeen instalments of Cap's UK run – for although a critical knockout, there just never seemed to be a sufficient audience to make his title viable. It begins with **Bad Moon Rising** – the aftermath of the classic **Jaspers Warp** storyline that had run the previous year (and which remains to my mind one of the most emotionally powerful stories Alan Moore has ever written) – and concludes with **Should Auld Acquaintance . . .** And what do you get along the way? The formal introduction and evolution of Cap's lover, Meggan. The Crazy Gang. Vixen. Gatecrasher and her Technet. The final confrontation between Cap and his arch-foe Slaymaster. Yet another Saturnyne. The Warpies. The RCX. King Croc and some shocking revelations about Brian's older brother, Jamie. Love and death, honour and glory, triumph and tragedy. And, of course, tea (and sympathy) at the Scott house.

Not to mention, some superb scripting by Jamie Delano – and last, but far from least, the art of Alan Davis.

When you create a character and a series – regardless of whether it's for yourself or a company, whether you own it or they do – a soft spot always remains. No matter how dumb the book or awkward the situation, these people are some small part of you and you can't ever look at them down the line (after you and they have parted

6

ways) without feeling some small twinge of nostalgia and perhaps a sense of sadness, because (in your heart of hearts) it isn't being done as well as you could do it, and you feel sorry for them because they're being so short-changed. But, occasionally, you come back to a character and series and discover quite the opposite. Whatever you did, whatever you had in mind when you set characters and events in motion, is nothing compared to what's happening today.

Such, to my delight, was the case with Cap. I almost didn't recognise Brian Braddock, and confess I never suspected he had such potential in him. Proud, headstrong (to a fault), heroic in spite of himself, painfully aware of his flaws, no less human for all his power and the responsibilities it thrusts upon him, he could be a royal pain in the butt, yet also someone a reader could empathise with and root for. I saw characters I'd created ages ago – such as Bri's twin sister, Betsy, and CID Commander Dai Thomas – totally changed, and all the better for it. I liked the people and I liked the book and my reaction at the end of each story was, what the heck comes next? And, being a greedy, acquisitive sod, I couldn't wait for the chance to play with them myself.

However, the lion's share of the credit must go to Alan Davis. One of the absolute joys of comics – as both a profession and an art form – is that it allows you to work in collaboration with other people. There's a school of thought which says that the creative process is best served when there is only a single artistic mind involved from start to finish – the same person writing and pencilling and inking a story, giving it an absolute coherence of vision. There's something to be said for that. But there is also something to be said for the collaborative effort. A synthesis of the talents and creative instincts of a writer, a penciller and an editor, wherein what emerges may not be the pristine product of a single mind but may instead –, when all the elements *click* – be a whole which is far greater than the sum of its parts. There's an excitement, an effervescence, to bouncing ideas off collaborators that quite frankly isn't there when you're working by yourself. Because that other mind, coming from different perceptions, with a different creative agenda, can quite suddenly take the story off in directions you might never have dreamed of – which in turn might spark you to go off on a completely different tangent yourself. In a collaboration, there's more of a sense of the unexpected. Out of the respect you hold for your collaborator, you want to do the

7

best possible work you're capable of – come up with a story that'll make him want to draw his socks off – so that when those inspired pencils come back to you for scripting, you pick up on the penciller's enthusiasm and try to match or top him with your script. Best pushing best pushing best – with the reader being the final benefactor.

In my career, I've had the ridiculous good fortune to work with many of the finest artists in the business. Without question, Alan Davis stands in the top rank, among the very best. Story-telling, characterisation, draftsmanship, imagination – he not only excels in every category, he gets better as he goes along. He's the kind of penciller of whom a writer can ask virtually anything – any setting, any emotion, any scene – with the supreme confidence that you'll get what you asked for, as well as, or better then, you imagined it. He can do an action sequence or a quiet scene, people in costumes or in civilian clothes, moments of high drama or base comedy, Earth or the furthest reaches of Outer Space (not to mention the Outer Hebrides), science fiction, super-heroes or fantasy human beings or alien critters. In fact, hyperbole aside, I've yet to discover anything he *can't* draw (and not for want of trying, either!) Every time I get to the end of each segment of pages he's sent me to write, I find myself frantic with anticipation to see what comes next. On top of that, he's one of the nicest, most considerate of people to work with – and that's a rare charm in an industry where unbridled lunacy is the norm.

So, in a very real sense, what you have here is about as good as this genre gets – top-notch stories, evocatively told, about people you care for and villains you can easily love to hate, with endings that move you. The power of simplicity. An entertainment.

Doesn't seem like all that much, really – till you try to do one yourself.

You see, the only thing more fun than reading Alan's work, is getting to work *with* him. The work of Dave Thorpe, Alan Moore and Jamie Delano – and Alan Davis himself, who wrote the last two issues (and that really was *not* a very nice thing to do to Betsy, Alan) – has blazed some pretty wild trails and set some pretty high standards. It's a challenge to live up to them.

And a pleasure.

CHRIS CLAREMONT
New York City
September 1988

MARCH 18TH 1984.

THE FULL MOON'S GENTLE LIGHT WASHES THE ROOFTOPS LIKE SILVER RAIN, SILHOUETTING A LONE FIGURE AGAINST LONDON'S GLITTERING SKYLINE.

HE HAS TRAVELLED THE COSMOS, HELPED SAVE THE UNIVERSE AND SEEN THINGS WE CAN ONLY DREAM OF. HE IS MORE THAN A MAN, HE IS A HERO...

Captain BRITAIN

BAD MOON RISING

"IT'S HARD TO BELIEVE JUST HOW PEACEFUL THINGS HAVE BEEN."

"SIX MONTHS AGO I FELT I WAS BEING DRIVEN MAD - SLAYMASTER, SATURNYNE, THE SPECIAL EXECUTIVE, JASPERS... AND THE FURY. SO MUCH HAS HAPPENED IN ONE SHORT YEAR."

"WELL, ALMOST EVERYONE... BETSY REMEMBERS."

"POOR BETSY, SHE STILL HASN'T FULLY RECOVERED FROM THE PSYCHIC SHOCK SHE FELT AS TOM LENNOX DIED."

"EVERYTHING HAS RETURNED TO NORMAL, JUST AS ROMA SAID. THE NATURAL ORDER OF THINGS WOULD NOT TOLERATE THE JASPERS WARP, REALITY IS REPAIRING ITSELF."

"EVERYONE HAS FORGOTTEN THE NIGHTMARE, IT'S LIKE AN EPIDEMIC OF AMNESIA."

"BUT NOW, NOW IT ALL SEEMS A LIFETIME AWAY."

"AND CAPTAIN UK. I HAVEN'T HEARD FROM LINDA SINCE WE ARRIVED BACK ON EARTH. SHE MUST BE AS BUSY AS I AM, ORGANISING HER LIFE, TRYING TO MAKE SOME SENSE OF IT ALL."

"FORTUNATELY, THE CAVERN COMPUTER HAS RECOVERED FROM THE FURY'S PSIONIC DRAIN, I'LL NEED ITS HELP TO GET THE ESTATE IN ORDER."

"BETSY AND ALISON WILL WANT TO STAY THERE AFTER THEIR RETREAT WITH VICTORIA BENTLEY."

"BUT HOW AM I GOING TO EXPLAIN THE MANOR'S RE-APPEARANCE WHEN I DROP THE HOLOGRAPHIC DEFENCE FIELD? AND EMMA?"

"WHAT AM I GOING TO DO ABOUT EMMA? A CHAR LADY WHO'S LOST SEVEN YEARS OF HER LIFE SERVING AN INVISIBLE COMPUTERISED HOUSE ..."

"IT'S NO GOOD... I THOUGHT A BREAK FROM THE MANOR MIGHT CLEAR MY HEAD, BUT THERE'S NO GETTING AWAY FROM IT..."

·HE REACTS WITHOUT HESITATION.

AIERRGH

EAGER TO USE HIS POWER.

ROOWR

TO FEEL THE THRILL HE'S LONGED FOR THROUGHOUT THESE IDLE MONTHS.

HE THROWS CAUTION TO THE WIND...

KREEEE

UF

AND IS TOSSED ASIDE BY A SNARLING TORNADO THAT EVAPORATES IN THE SPECTRAL GLOOM.

ARE YOU OKAY? DID THAT THING HURT YOU?

GERROF, I'M ALRIGHT, JUST NEED A DRINK TO STEADY ME NERVES. IT WERE ONE A'THEM SNIFFER KIDS, STUFF TURNS 'EM INTA MANIACS IT DOES.

NEAR SCARED ME T'DEATH HE DID! TRIED TO KILL ME, CLAWIN' AND BITIN' LIKE A BLEEDIN' ANIMAL!

NO, WHATEVER IT WAS THAT ATTACKED YOU, IT WASN'T HUMAN.

IT WAS TOO FAST, TOO STRONG, IT ALMOST BROKE MY RIBS — NOT EVEN A CRAZED HUMAN IS THAT STRONG!

AN JUST WOT D'YA THINK YOU ARE, Y'BIG PONCE?

THINK YOU'RE A SUPER'ERO OR SOMETHIN'?

I'D SUGGEST YOU LEAVE AND FIND SOMEWHERE TO SPEND THE NIGHT.

I'M GOING AFTER IT... WHATEVER IT WAS.

THERE Y'GO, 'CLEAR OFF' HE SEZ, IT'S ALWAYS THE SAME, NO ONE CARES.

THERE IS ONLY THE MOON,

THE MOON AND THE PAIN,

THE PAIN AND THE RAGE.

SKREEEEE

"IT'S HIM! THE CAPTAIN!"

THROUGH THE SEARING SCARLET HAZE, SHE REMEMBERS.

NO, NOT YOU.

NOOOOOO

WAIT! COME BACK!

BUT SHE'S GONE. A SILENT SHADOW... SWALLOWED BY THE MUTE DARKNESS.

"WHY DID SHE RUN? SHE SEEMED TO RECOGNISE ME JUST BEFORE SHE STOPPED ATTACKING... SHE WAS TERRIFIED... BUT WHY?"

"SHE WASN'T TRYING TO ESCAPE, I CAN STILL SENSE HER PRESENCE NEARBY."

"BUT IT'S NOT AS IF SHE'S PREPARING TO ATTACK AGAIN."

"SHE'S JUST WATCHING."

WATCHING.

WATCHING?

CHINK!

ALRIGHT! WHO THE...

WHO ARE YOU?

MICKY... AND SHE'S MY SISTER, JOSIE... IT'S MEGGAN. SHE... WE... WE...

WE LOOK AFTER MEGGAN. SHE LIVES HERE, SHE HAS DONE FOR MONTHS, WE'RE HER FRIENDS.

WE BRING HER THINGS AND HELP TO KEEP HER CALM WHEN THE MOON'S FULL.

MEGGAN? WHEN THE MOON'S FULL...?

YOU MEAN SHE'S A WERE-WOLF?

DON'T BE SILLY, SHE SAYS SHE'S A MUTANT, LIKE THEY HAVE IN AMERICA, BUT THE FULL MOON MAKES HER GO A BIT CRAZY.

SHE'S NICE REALLY, BUT THAT TRAMP, SHE SAID HE STANK, LIKE A DEAD ANIMAL.

SHE COULDN'T BEAR IT, SHE JUST WENT WILD.

15

SHE WATCHES FROM THE DARK, THROUGH THE BLINDING PAIN.

SHE IS CONFUSED, AND THE CONFUSION HURTS.

SKREEEEE

WAIT!

SHE SEES THE CAPTAIN AND HER FRIENDS, BUT HE IS HURTING THEM.

MEGGAN? THE FULL? MEAN...A WOLF?

MEGGAN...HERE DONE MONTHS. WE FRIENDS THINGS TO CALM MOON...SILLY MUTANT HAVE IN GO MOON A CRAZY NICE STANK DEAD...WILD.

HE'S THE HERO, BUT HE'S HURTING HER FRIENDS.

MEGGAN! STOP...

PLEASE, MEGGAN, STOP!

BUT SHE CAN NO LONGER HEAR, SHE HAS SUCCUMBED TO THE PAIN THAT CLOUDS HER SENSES.

THERE IS ONLY THE PAIN.

THRUUNG

SKREEEK

RUN, MICKY!

MICKY... MICKY'S DEAD.

NOOOOO!!

MEGGAN ...WAIT!

AAAAAAA

MICKY!!

HE HAS TRAVELLED THE COSMOS, HELPED SAVE THE UNIVERSE AND SEEN THINGS WE CAN ONLY DREAM OF. HE IS MORE THAN A MAN, HE IS A HERO.

OR SO HE HAD THOUGHT, UNTIL TONIGHT.

GRADANG

17

Tea and Sympathy

MRS SCOTT... I'M SORRY TO INTRUDE... I'VE COME TO APOLOGISE.

I'M RESPONSIBLE FOR YOUR SON'S DEATH.

NO YOU'RE NOT. I LOST MICKY A LONG TIME AGO.

HE GOT IN WITH THE WRONG CROWD WHEN HIS DAD LEFT US... IT WAS ONLY A MATTER OF TIME.

YOU'D BETTER COME IN.

THE FEW NEIGHBOURS LEFT LIVING IN THIS SLUM WILL BE WONDERING WHAT'S GOING ON.

ER... THANK YOU, MRS SCOTT.

JOAN. CALL ME JOAN.

OH, RIGHT...

JOSIE YOU KNOW, AND THIS IS MY FATHER-IN-LAW, BOB.

PLEASED TO MEET YOU, LAD... SIT YOURSELF DOWN.

I'VE READ A LOT ABOUT YOU, CAPTAIN. YOU'VE BEEN FRONT PAGE NEWS EVERY DAY THIS WEEK, "BRITAIN'S OWN SUPERHERO BACK IN ACTION" AND BACK WITH A VENGEANCE, I'D SAY.

AND WHAT ABOUT THAT BIG ARMED ROBBERY YOU STOPPED?

EE, IT MADE ME PROUD TO BE BRITISH, THE WAY YOU SORTED THEM RUFFIANS OUT.

AND YOU'D ONLY JUST GOT BACK AFTER SPENDING OVER NINE HOURS CLEARING THAT MOTORWAY OF THE PILE-UP WRECKAGE. **CHAMPION.**

YOU SAVED THEM FORTY KIDS WHEN THEIR SCHOOL BURNT DOWN AND THEN THAT PLANE LOAD OF HOSTAGES FROM THOSE LIBERATION WHATSIT TERRORISTS.

THE COUNTRY NEEDS SOMEONE LIKE YOU, CAPTAIN.

TROUBLE WITH FOLK TODAY IS NO PATRIOTISM. NO PRIDE. IT WEREN'T LIKE THAT WHEN I WAS A LAD.

DAD... DON'T NAG.

OH NO, KING AND COUNTRY, THAT'S WHAT MATTERED. WE WERE A NATION. WE DIDN'T GO CAP IN HAND TO ANY COMMON MARKET BEGGING FOR HANDOUTS.

OH... SORRY, LOVE.

WOULD YOU LIKE A CUP OF TEA, CAPTAIN?

YES, I WOULD, THANK YOU. THAT WOULD BE VERY NICE.

WE HAVEN'T HEARD MUCH OF YOU IN THE PAST SIX YEARS, CAPTAIN. HAVE YOU BEEN IN AMERICA ... I MEAN, WHILE YOU'VE BEEN AWAY. THAT'S WHERE ALL THE SUPERHEROES GO, ISN'T IT?

NO, I'VE BEEN IN BRITAIN. WELL, I HAVE BEEN FOR THE LAST SIX MONTHS. BEFORE THAT, THINGS WERE ...

WHY WEREN'T YOU BACK IN ACTION, THEN? A LOT OF FOLK NEEDED YOU ...

WE COULD HAVE DONE WITHOUT HIM!

YOU'RE JUST LIKE ALL THE OTHER ESTABLISHMENT STOOGES! YOU INTERFERE WITH EVERYONE BECAUSE YOU THINK YOU KNOW BETTER! YOU THINK YOU CAN RUN THEIR LIVES BECAUSE YOU'VE GOT SOME POWER!

JOSIE! DON'T YOU DARE SPEAK TO ANYONE LIKE THAT!

NO, PLEASE, SHE'S RIGHT.

FOR THE LAST THREE YEARS I'VE RUBBED SHOULDERS WITH COSMIC BEINGS, FIGHTING TO SAVE THE UNIVERSE.

I'D FORGOTTEN MY RESPONSIBILITY TO ORDINARY PEOPLE.

I DIDN'T THINK THEY WERE MY PROBLEM. I THOUGHT I'D RISEN ABOVE THEM.

I'M AFRAID THAT IT'S TAKEN YOUR SON'S DEATH TO MAKE ME REALISE HOW WRONG I'VE BEEN.

YOU'RE BEING TOO HARD ON YOURSELF, CAPTAIN.

AM I, MRS SCOTT? I WAS CARELESS, I KNEW YOUR CHILDREN WERE NEARBY, BUT I IGNORED THE OBVIOUS DANGER TO THEM. I WAS MORE INTENT ON BEATING THAT CREATURE... MEGGAN.

AND ALL I WANTED TO DO WAS KILL YOU.

MEGGAN...

GOOD LORD.

YOU'VE COME BACK.

I'VE NEVER BEEN TOO FAR AWAY, JOSIE.

I WATCHED THE HOUSE EVER SINCE THE NIGHT MICKY DIED. I WANTED TO BE NEAR YOU, TO EXPLAIN... BUT I WAS SCARED.

I SEEN THE POLICE WHEN THEY CAME, AND ALL YOUR FRIENDS... AND THE UNDERTAKERS.

YOU WERE ALL SO UPSET. I COULDN'T FACE YOU.

BUT THEN I SEEN THE CAPTAIN, SO I'VE BEEN LISTENING OUTSIDE.

IT WASN'T HIS FAULT YOU KNOW, IT'S MINE. BUT I SWEAR I'VE NEVER LOST CONTROL LIKE THAT BEFORE. I JUST COULDN'T HELP MYSELF.

IT WAS THE SMELL OF THE TRAMP. I DON'T KNOW WHY, BUT IT MADE ME FEEL THREATENED. I'M NOT USUALLY THAT CRAZY, HONESTLY.

IT WAS THE SMELL.

21

MICKY'S DEAD! BLAMING YOURSELVES WON'T BRING HIM BACK, **NOTHING** WILL.

LOOK AT YOURSELF, CAPTAIN, YOU'RE EXHAUSTED-AND LITTLE WONDER, YOU'VE BEEN INVOLVED IN NO AMOUNT OF RESCUES AND SCUFFLES THIS WEEK.

I ACCEPTED THE POWERS, MRS SCOTT, THEY CARRY RESPONSIBILITIES I CAN NO LONGER IGNORE.

ARE YOU SURE YOU HAVEN'T JUST BEEN TRYING TO MAKE UP FOR FEELING GUILTY?

I AM GUILTY.

I FAILED TO HELP YOUR SON, I **WON'T** FAIL ANYONE AGAIN.

BUT NO MATTER HOW POWERFUL YOU ARE CAPTAIN, YOU **CAN'T** SHOULDER THE WORLD'S PROBLEMS, YOU'RE STILL ONLY **ONE** MAN.

YOU HAVE TO **LIVE** YOUR LIFE AND HELP OTHERS ALONG THE WAY. THAT'S ALL **ANY** OF US CAN DO.

THE POLICE AND THE COURTS WERE SATISFIED IT WAS AN ACCIDENT.

WHY CAN'T **YOU** ACCEPT IT.

I HAVE!

MRS SCOTT...

PLEASE, MEGGAN. YOU'RE JOSIE'S FRIEND, AND AS SUCH YOU'RE WELCOME IN THIS HOUSE...

EVEN IF YOU DO LOOK A BIT WEIRD.

I'LL SAY.

PLEASE SIT DOWN, CAPTAIN AND HAVE ANOTHER CUP OF TEA.

AND MAYBE YOU COULD TELL US ALL ABOUT THOSE "COSMIC BEINGS" YOU SAVED THE UNIVERSE WITH.

THEY SMILE, WARM, GENUINE SMILES.

AND THOUGH THE GRIEF AND GUILT REMAIN, IT BECOMES A LITTLE EASIER TO BEAR.

TIME PASSES. THE TEA IS DRUNK AND THE BISCUITS EATEN.

...YOU SEEM TO BE VERY FOND OF THIS SATURNYNE, CAPTAIN.

SOUNDS A BIT HARD-BOILED TO ME.

WELL, ER... SHE'S CERTAINLY A VERY... UNIQUE...

HA HA, HE'S BLUSHING!

LAUGHTER GREETS THE EVENING.

AND HE IS SUDDENLY AWARE THAT IT IS THE SOUND OF HIS OWN LAUGHTER. IT FEELS GOOD.

IT'S BEEN SUCH A LONG TIME SINCE HE'S LAUGHED.

...SUCH A LONG TIME SINCE HE'S BEEN WITH ORDINARY PEOPLE.

HE HAD FORGOTTEN THE SIMPLE PLEASURES OF A FAMILY AND FRIENDS.

...I'VE NEVER MET ANY ALIENS, CAPTAIN, I'M THE WEIRDEST CREATURE I KNOW.

MIND YOU, WHAT REALLY IS WEIRD, IS HOW I'VE MANAGED TO LOSE MY FOLKS. THEY ARE TRAVELLERS, YOU SEE.

IT HAPPENED ABOUT SIX MONTHS AGO, I THINK.

I CAN'T EVEN REMEMBER WHY I LEFT THEM. WHEN-EVER I TRY TO, I SEE THIS SORT OF CONCENTRATION CAMP. AND THE SKY'S FUNNY TOO... ALL GREEN AND TWISTED. IT'S CRAZY...

YOU REMEMBER.

REMEMBER WHAT?

IT'S A LONG STORY, MEGGAN, BUT I MAY BE ABLE TO HELP YOU TRACE YOUR FAMILY.

I HAVE A FAIRLY LARGE...'HEADQUARTERS' IN THE COUNTRY, AND ACCESS TO A RATHER SPECIAL COMPUTER.

I'D BE PLEASED TO HAVE YOU STAY UNTIL I DID. YOU'D BE MORE COMFORT-ABLE THAN YOU WERE IN THAT OLD WARE-HOUSE...

SECRET HEAD-QUARTERS, WOWIE!!

LAUGHTER.

A PITY IT NEVER LASTS.

MORE IMPORTANTLY, WHERE DID THEY COME FROM?

AND WHY DID THEY ATTACK AT THIS PARTICULAR TIME AND PLACE?

WE SHOWED THEM OFF THOUGH, THEY WON'T BE BACK IN A HURRY!

LET'S HOPE NOT.

YEAH, WE NEARLY DEMOLISHED THE SCOTTS' HOUSE AS IT IS.

OH NO!

JOAN! ARE YOU ALRIGHT?

AND JOSIE AND MR SCOTT, WERE THEY HURT?

NO, WE'RE ALL FINE.

A BIT RATTLED, BUT THEN WE'RE NOT USED TO ALL THIS EXCITEMENT.

IT'S BEEN A REALLY HECTIC DAY. THE NEIGHBOURS WILL NEVER BELIEVE IT.

I'M NOT SURE I DO.

I DON'T KNOW WHAT TO SAY... I'M JUST SO SORRY.

I CAME TO APOLOGISE, TO MAKE AMENDS, INSTEAD I'VE MADE THINGS WORSE.

I'VE DESTROYED YOUR HOME.

REALLY, CAPTAIN, YOU WERE DEFENDING YOURSELF, YOU CAN'T TAKE ALL THE BLAME. ANYWAY, TRY TO LOOK ON THE BRIGHT SIDE OF THINGS.

BUT YOUR HOUSE, IT'S RUINED.

AND THAT MEANS THE COUNCIL WILL HAVE TO RE-HOUSE US.

WE'LL BE OUT OF THIS SLUM AT LAST.

MORE TEA, ANYBODY?

25

JUNE 6TH, 1984.

In All The Old Familiar Places...

OH BRIAN! I'M **SO** GLAD TO BE HOME.

IT'S GOOD TO HAVE YOU BACK, BETSY.

YOU TOO, ALISON, HOW ARE YOU? YOU LOOK WELL.

I AM VERY WELL, THANK YOU, BRIAN.

VICTORIA BENTLEY POSSESSES REMARKABLE SKILLS, MY HEALTH IMPROVES DAILY.

MISS BETSY...

OO, MISS BETSY, YOU'RE BACK, AND YOU LOOK LOVELY, JUST LOVELY...

EMMA, YOU'RE...

BACK TO NORMAL. I'LL EXPLAIN LATER.

...A LITTLE PEEKY, MAYBE, BUT I'LL SOON FATTEN YOU UP. I'VE BAKED A CAKE, YOUR FAVOURITE, WALNUT CREAM.

DON'T FUSS, EMMA...

AND DON'T SAY YOU'RE DIETING, FASHION MODELS, YOU'RE ALL THE SAME, ALWAYS DIETING.

BRIAN! HURRY UP, YOU'RE ON TELLY NEXT.

WHO...?

THAT'S MEGGAN.

SHE'S STAYING HERE FOR A WHILE, BUT I'D BETTER WARN YOU, SHE'S...

27

...AND HERE RECENTLY RETURNED FROM A WORLD TOUR IS BRIAN BRADDOCK.

NOW TELL ME, HOW IS THE RECONSTRUCTION WORK ON THE MANOR PROGRESSING?

VERY WELL, VERY WELL INDEED. OF COURSE, THE EXTENT OF THE DAMAGE WAS NOT AS GREAT AS WAS ORIGINALLY FEARED...

...I INTEND TO RE-OPEN THE ESTATE'S FARMS AND PUT ALL THE LAND TO GOOD USE.

UNEMPLOYMENT IS FAR MORE THAN A POLITICAL ISSUE IN THIS PART OF THE COUNTRY. YOUR DECISION HAS BEEN WELCOMED BY MANY UNEMPLOYED FAMILIES IN NEIGHBOURING VILLAGES.

BRIAN!

WELL, I DIDN'T SAY WHICH WORLDS.

THERE WASN'T ANY DAMAGE, WAS THERE, BRIAN?

NO, NOT FROM THE S.T.R.I.K.E. BOMBING, BUT THE FORCE OF SMASHING THE FURY INTO THE UNDERGROUND CAVERNS CAUSED SOME SUBSIDENCE.

THE COMPUTER IS TAKING CARE OF IT.

BRIAN, HOW COME THE TELLY CAN SEE MEN REBUILDING THE MANOR WHEN IT DOESN'T NEED TO BE REBUILT?

THEY AREN'T ACTUALLY THERE, MEGGAN.

REMEMBER I TOLD YOU HOW THE CAVERN COMPUTER CREATED A HOLOGRAPHIC IMAGE OF THE MANOR WHEN IT WAS ATTACKED?

YEAH, THE MISSILES "HIT" THE IMAGE, THEN THE COMPUTER MADE IT LOOK LIKE THE MANOR WAS IN RUINS.

SO?

WELL, NOW THE COMPUTER HAS CREATED FAKE MEN WITH PHONEY MACHINES TO REBUILD A PRETEND HOUSE. AND WHEN IT'S REBUILT, WE CAN DROP THE HOLOGRAPHIC SCREEN.

...THE MANOR SHOULD BE FULLY RENOVATED IN THE NEXT EIGHTEEN MONTHS.

OO, WEREN'T YOU GOOD, MASTER BRIAN.

YEAH, YOU WERE GREAT. IT MUST BE NICE TO BE SO FAMOUS.

I HOPE ALL GOES WELL. THANK YOU FOR YOUR TIME, MR BRADDOCK.

THANK YOU.

CROSSROADS

HEY, MAYBE YOU'LL BE SPOTTED FOR A PART IN CROSSROADS.

I THINK THAT'S OUR CUE TO GO AND TRY SOME OF EMMA'S CAKE, BETSY.

OVER A YEAR AGO, IN A WORLD YET TO TWIST AND DARKEN, HE HAD WALKED THESE CORRIDORS WITH A WOMAN FROM AN EARTH THAT DIED.

THEY SPOKE OF THE FUTURE, OF THE FEAR.

OF THE ANARCHY, AND THE DEATH.

THAT TIME HAS PASSED, BUT THE NIGHTMARE LINGERS.

...VICTORIA MADE ME STRONG AGAIN. BUT I CAN'T FORGET...

...ALL OF THE JASPERS' MADNESS... THE REALITY WARP... THE CAMP...

LOSING TOM. IT STILL HURTS.

WE WERE PSYCHICALLY LINKED WHEN HE DIED.

I FELT HIS DEATH, WRENCHING... EMPTY.

NOW, YOU SAID YOU WOULD EXPLAIN ABOUT EMMA.

YES. WE KNEW THE COMPUTER HAD ORIGINALLY BRAINWASHED EMMA TO SERVE IT AND THAT SHE HAD GROWN TO RELY ON IT FOR SOME PRETTY BASIC FUNCTIONS.

WHICH IS WHY WE HAD TO LEAVE HER IN ITS CARE WHEN WE FLED TO LONDON.

WHAT WE DIDN'T REALISE WAS THAT, SOMEHOW, THE COMPUTER HAD GROWN "FOND" OF EMMA.

IT TOOK ALMOST SIX WEEKS TO RELEASE HER FROM ITS CONTROL.

THE PROBLEM WAS TO RESTORE THE ABILITY FOR VOLUNTARY ACTION, HER BASIC INDIVIDUALITY, WITHOUT CAUSING TRAUMA FROM THE SEPARATION.

SHE DOESN'T REMEMBER ANYTHING ABOUT HER ENSLAVEMENT, BUT HAS OCCASIONALLY COMPLAINED OF A FEELING OF LOSS...

LIKE THE DEATH OF A DEAR FRIEND. I CAN'T REALLY EXPLAIN IT.

THEY HAD BEEN TOGETHER FOR SEVEN YEARS, BRIAN, AND THEY WERE ALONE. THE OUTSIDE WORLD BELIEVED THE MANOR WAS DESTROYED. IT MUST HAVE BEEN A BIT LIKE BEING MARRIED.

MAYBE. ANYWAY, SHE SEEMS TO BE CONTENT TO STAY AT THE MANOR, EVEN THOUGH MEGGAN WORRIES HER A BIT AND THERE ARE SOME "WEIRD GOINGS ON."

SHE HAS NOWHERE ELSE TO GO, NO LIVING RELATIVES. SHE'S ALWAYS LIVED HERE, EVER SINCE WE WERE KIDS, IT'S HER HOME. SHE'S ONE OF THE FAMILY.

BRIAN!

WHO... WHAT ARE THEY?

IT'S ALRIGHT, BETSY. THEY ARE THE COMPUTER'S SOLID LIGHT HOLOGRAMS, REPAIRING THE SUBSIDENCE DAMAGE I MENTIONED EARLIER.

SOLID-LIGHT HOLOGRAMS?

YES, JUST LIKE THE COMPUTER'S PHYSICAL PROJECTION MASTERMIND.

THAT WAS THE LASER-FIRING GIANT WHICH ATTACKED ME WHEN I FIRST DISCOVERED THE MANOR WAS INTACT BEHIND THE HOLOGRAPHIC FIELD.

THESE ARE MORE SOPHISTICATED.

AND FRIENDLY, NOW THAT THE COMPUTER'S ON OUR SIDE!

I DON'T REALLY UNDERSTAND THE PHYSICS INVOLVED, BUT...

BETSY?

HAVE YOU EVER WONDERED HOW DAD COULD CONSTRUCT A COMPUTER, MORE THAN TEN YEARS AGO, THAT IS FAR IN ADVANCE OF MODERN TECHNOLOGY...

WHAT DO THOSE ONES DO, BRIAN?

NOT AGAIN.

SURRENDER!

STAY BACK, BETSY.

HE HAD BEEN CAUGHT OFF-GUARD.

WITHOUT HIS UNIFORM, THE AMPLIFIER OF LATENT PROWESS.

BUT CLOTHES MAKETH NOT THE MAN...

OR THE HERO.

AKK!

SKAGGED HIM.

WHO ARE YOU? WHY ARE YOU TRYING TO KILL ME?

BOUNTY! BIG NUMBERS FOR KAPTAIN BRITON!

NOW WE-SORTS FRY TARGET BRAIN. STILL HIM!

AG!

NO!!

ZEEEEEEET.

THEY'RE GONE, BETSY. ARE YOU ALRIGHT?

I WILL BE... JUST DRAINED.

HOW... WHAT DID YOU DO?

I'VE GROWN, BRIAN. VICTORIA SHOWED ME HOW TO USE TOM'S DEATH...

...WHO WERE YOUR ATTACKERS?

I DON'T KNOW. THEY ATTACKED ME ONCE BEFORE AND DISAPPEARED JUST AS QUICKLY...

I HAD JUST MET A REALLY REMARKABLE WOMAN, JOAN SCOTT...

SHE MADE ME THINK...ACCEPT MY SITUATION, MY RESPONSIBILITIES.

I HAD STARTED TO BELIEVE I COULD LEAD A NORMAL LIFE,

BUT NOW...

NOW I HAVE A HORRIBLE FEELING THAT THINGS ARE BEGINNING TO GO WRONG AGAIN.

CHIEF INSPECTOR
DAI THOMAS
82

CAPTAIN BRITAIN
BRIAN BRADDOCK
5/334/17

PERHAPS IT IS HIS IMAGINATION...

BUT IT IS AS IF SOMETHING HAS HAPPENED WHICH NO ONE CAN RECOGNISE.

THERE IS A TIREDNESS UNDER THE OPPRESSION OF THE SKY.

DO GO STRAIGHT IN, CHIEF INSPECTOR THOMAS.

THE GENTLEMEN **ARE** READY FOR YOU.

THE GENTLEMEN, HIS SUPERIORS.

AH, CHIEF INSPECTOR, DO SIT DOWN.

WILL YOU TAKE SOME TEA?

THANK YOU, SIR. I DON'T MIND IF I DO.

IF YOU WILL BEAR WITH ME, GENTLEMEN, I HAVE SOME SLIDES TO SHOW YOU.

PLEASE PROCEED AS YOU SEE FIT. YOU HAVE OUR COMPLETE ATTENTION.

I'M SURE THAT YOU WILL ALL RECOGNISE OUR LOCAL SUPERHERO, CURRENTLY THE DARLING OF THE MEDIA.

INDEED, HE HAS BEEN OF VALUABLE ASSISTANCE TO THE AUTHORITIES OF LATE.

Captain BRITAIN

PICTURES PUZZLES & PAWNS

JAMIE DELANO & ALAN DAVIS -CO-CREATORS

STEVE CRADDOCK -LETTERER

YOU INDICATED THAT YOU HAD NEW AND IMPORTANT EVIDENCE.

I HOPE THAT WE ARE NOT TO BE TREATED TO ANOTHER EPISODE OF YOUR SOMEWHAT OBSESSIVE ANTIPATHY TOWARDS BEINGS OF THIS KIND.

THE DEATH OF YOUR WIFE WAS TRAGIC.

BUT IT **WAS** AN ACCIDENT.

HE REMEMBERS HER FACE.

SOFT AND EMPTY UNDER THE HARD, BRUTAL CONCRETE AS THE BATTLING SUPERBEINGS MOVED ON, CARELESSLY OBLIVIOUS OF THE LIFE SNUFFED OUT IN THEIR WAKE.

YES, AN ACCIDENT.

AND ACCIDENTS WILL HAPPEN. THEY HAVE HAPPENED BEFORE...

DAILY Mirror

1984   17p

TEENAGER CRUSHED IN WAREHOUSE TRAGEDY

victim MICKY SCOTT

...THEY ARE STARTING TO HAPPEN AGAIN.

HE BURIES HIS WIFE'S MEMORY AND TURNS TO THE FACTS.

VERY WELL. LET US MOVE TO ANOTHER FACE THAT HAS BEEN IN THE NEWS, ALTHOUGH FOR DIFFERENT REASONS.

THIS IS THE FACE OF **BRIAN BRADDOCK.**

CENTRAL RECORDS TELL US THAT BRIAN BRADDOCK WAS BORN, WITH HIS TWIN SISTER ELIZABETH, IN THE EARLY HOURS OF APRIL 23RD 1956.

THE ORIGINS OF HIS PARENTS ARE HARDER TO TRACE, WE HAVE NO RECORD OF THEM PRIOR TO 1945, WHEN THEY PURCHASED BRADDOCK MANOR.

OF COURSE, IT IS **POSSIBLE** THAT RECORDS WERE LOST IN THE WAR.

...ALTHOUGH ELDER BROTHER JAMIE IS ALSO UNLISTED UNTIL HIS NAME WAS PUT DOWN FOR HARROW IN 1948.

A BIT OF A TEARAWAY WAS JAMIE. HE'S A RACING DRIVER NOW.

YOUNG BRIAN, THOUGH, WAS A HORSE OF A DIFFERENT COLOUR. HE WAS QUIET AND STUDIOUS, WITH A KEEN SCIENTIFIC BRAIN.

Daily Telegraph

SCIENTIST DIES IN FREAK ELECTRICAL ACCIDENT

Local power cut for four hours

One of Britain's most respected research scientists, Dr. James Braddock died last night, along with his wife, Elizabeth in an explosion which wrecked the private laboratory at his home, Braddock Manor, and brought a loss of mains power to several hundred homes in the vicinity. The power cut lasted for four hours. The precise cause of the accident has not yet been defined, but early unconfirmed reports suggested that both the doctor and Mrs Braddock were in the laboratory at the time of the explosion.

The Braddocks are survived by three children: the elder son, Jamie is a well-known racing car driver, while the twins, Brian and Elizabeth are both at college...

...DOUBTLESS INHERITED FROM HIS FATHER, WHO WAS A BIT OF A RECLUSE.

HE DIED IN A LABORATORY ACCIDENT AT BRADDOCK MANOR.

BY 1976, IN ADVANCE OF HIS YEARS, BRADDOCK WAS A GRADUATE STUDENT AT THAMES UNIVERSITY.

UP UNTIL NOW HE HAD LED A NORMAL, IF SOMEWHAT SECLUDED, LIFE.

NO YOUTHFUL INDISCRETIONS. NO STUDENT POLITICS. MR. NICE GUY, IN FACT.

YES, GENTLEMEN. IT'S ALWAYS THE QUIET ONES.

FORGIVE THE INTERRUPTION, CHIEF INSPECTOR, BUT ARE YOU PROPOSING A LINK BETWEEN BRADDOCK AND CAPTAIN BRITAIN?

HEIGHT- 6 foot 6 ins

WEIGHT- 18 stone approx.

MUSCULAR PHYSIQUE- ABNORMALLY developed

NECK - Sternomastoid/ Trapelius
SHOULDER- Deltoid
BACK- Latissimus Dorsi

SYNCHRONIC ANALYSIS-
1. Spontaneous use and application of correct grammar
2. Familiar use of technical and scientific terms
3. Pronunciation and grammatical definition suggest London (Thames) University education
4. No colloquial slang
5. No unusual inflections

SHALLOW PHILTRUM

SCARRED TUBERCLE

FAIR SKIN

LOW WING (ALA)

THIN NOSTRIL

DROPPED MEDIAL INCISOR

SCARRED MENTO-LOBIAL FURRO

I AM PROPOSING THAT BRIAN BRADDOCK IS CAPTAIN BRITAIN.

IT IS WARM BY THE FIRE.

WHAT'S THIS, BRIAN? NOT WAITING TO SEE YOURSELF ON THE BOX AGAIN, ARE YOU?

HELLO, BETSY!

IT MUST BE NICE TO BE SO FAMOUS.

BRIAN BRADDOCK, THE YOUNG SQUIRE RETURNED...

C'MON, YOU KNOW THAT THE ONLY REASON I'VE PUT MYSELF IN THE PUBLIC EYE IS TO SECURE OUR COVER.

NOT THROUGH VANITY, I ASSURE YOU.

DON'T GET ALL UPTIGHT. I WAS ONLY TEASING.

WE COULD BOTH DO WITH A BIT OF RELAXATION. I'VE JUST BEEN UP WITH MEGGAN— I DON'T THINK SHE'S USED TO BEING IN SUCH A BIG BUILDING YET.

WHAT ABOUT ALISON? HOW'S SHE?

STILL SLEEPING MOST OF THE TIME, BUT I THINK SHE'S IMPROVING.

IT'S GOOD TO BE WITH YOU AGAIN, BEE.

BEE?

WE USED TO CALL EACH OTHER THAT, DIDN'T WE, WHEN WE WERE KIDS.

IT SEEMS A LONG TIME AGO NOW. EVERYTHING SEEMS SO LONG AGO.

EVERYTHING BEFORE....

...BEFORE I LOST YOU FROM MY MIND.

BEFORE DARKMOOR!

IT WAS LONELY WITHOUT YOU, I DIDN'T KNOW WHAT WAS HAPPENING TO YOU. I WAS SCARED...

I WAS SCARED TOO...

"I WENT TO DARKMOOR TO HELP DR. TRAVIS IN THE SUMMER BREAK TO KEEP MYSELF BUSY AFTER MUM AND DAD DIED, AND TO GET SOME EXPERIENCE IN THE FIELD."

"IT DIDN'T SEEM AS IF I'D BEEN THERE FOR TEN MINUTES BEFORE THE CALM ORDER OF SCIENTIFIC RESEARCH WAS TRANSFORMED INTO SOMETHING MORE LIKE A JAMES BOND MOVIE..."

"I GOT EXPERIENCE ALRIGHT, BUT NOT THE KIND I EXPECTED."

"...ONLY THIS WAS FOR REAL."

THE FIRST RECORDED INCIDENT INVOLVING CAPTAIN BRITAIN TOOK PLACE IN THE LATE SUMMER OF 1976...

THE DESTRUCTION OF THE NUCLEAR RESEARCH COMPLEX ON DARKMOOR.

POLICE FILES ARE SLIM ON THIS SUBJECT, MoD HAD CONTROL OF THE FOLLOW-UP, AND SECURITY WAS...UH... EFFICIENT.

WE DO KNOW THAT BRADDOCK WAS PRESENT AT THE TIME.

PERHAPS IT WAS MERELY COINCIDENCE THAT CAPTAIN BRITAIN SHOULD CHOOSE THIS OCCASION TO STAGE HIS GRAND ENTRANCE...

...OR PERHAPS IT WAS NOT.

WHATEVER! THERE WAS NOW A NEW FORCE IN OUR MIDST.

WHITE HORSE

THE GUARDIAN

'Super Patriot' is threat says Dai Thomas

ENGLAND'S OWN SUPERHERO

UNFORTUNATELY, WHEREVER SUPER-HEROES APPEAR, SUPERVILLIANS ARISE TO CON-FRONT THEM.

THEIR POWERS ARE GREAT...THEY CAUSE DAMAGE. INNOCENT PEOPLE GET HURT...

...GET KILLED.

WE'VE SEEN IT IN THE STATES... WE'VE SEEN IT HERE.

IT'S STARTING AGAIN.

WITH DUE RESPECT, THE POLITICS OF THE RELATIONSHIP BETWEEN SUPERHEROES AND THE WORLD WHICH THEY INHABIT IS NOT OUR CONCERN HERE!

KINDLY CONFINE YOUR- SELF TO THE FACTS.

YES SIR.

THE FACTS, SIR.

FACT! BRADDOCK RETURNS TO UNIVERSITY.

CAPTAIN BRITAIN IS ACTIVE IN THE U.K.,

MY REPORT LISTS BRADDOCK FAMILY CONNECTIONS IN MANY CAPTAIN BRITAIN INCIDENTS, INCLUDING THE EVENTS WHICH CULMINATED IN THE BOMBING OF BRAD- DOCK MANOR BY S.T.R.I.K.E.

FACT! BRADDOCK VISITS AMERICA,

TIME

BRITISH SUPERHERO

AT THE SAME TIME, CAPTAIN BRITAIN IS CONSORTING WITH SUPERHEROES IN THE U.S.

FACT! WHILST FLYING BACK FROM KENNEDY AIRPORT, BRADDOCK'S PLANE GETS INTO TROUBLE...

EYEWITNESS REPORTS TELL US THAT HE JUMPS FROM THE PLANE SCREAMING THAT HE IS UNDER PSYCHIC ATTACK!

Daily Mail

THREE SURVIVE AIRLINE DISASTER

FACT! BRADDOCK IS MISSING, PRESUMED DEAD, AND CAPTAIN BRITAIN IS NO LONGER A FEATURE OF BRITISH LIFE.

FACT! FOUR YEARS LATER, WHEN ELIZABETH BRADDOCK, NOW WORKING FOR S.T.R.I.K.E., IS IN DANGER...

CAPTAIN BRITAIN REAPPEARS. HE IS BIGGER, MORE POWERFUL AND MORE DANGEROUS.

THE PSI-DIVISION OF THE ILL- FATED AGENCY S.T.R.I.K.E. IS UNDER ATTACK BY THE VIXEN'S ASSASSIN SLAYMASTER.

ELIZABETH BRADDOCK IS RESCUED BY A SUPER- BEING, WHO SLAYMASTER REVEALS, DURING INTERROGATION, TO BE CAPTAIN BRITAIN,

HS/743/SM.

HALF OF DENMARK STREET IS LAID WASTE IN THE CONFLICT.

HARDLY SUR- PRISING THAT SIR JAMES JASPERS GOT SO MUCH SUPPORT IN HIS STAND AGAINST SUPERHEROES, IS IT?

WHO?

YOU LIKED IT!

HOW COULD YOU LIKE IT?

IT'S THE **THRILL**, BETSY, IT'S THE **ADVENTURE.**

IT'S THE POWER AND THE GLORY SINGING IN THE VEINS.

IN THOSE EARLY DAYS I JUST USED TO FIGHT AND WIN...

"MY MIND WAS NOT FLEXIBLE ENOUGH FOR THE CONCEPTS INVOLVED, I THOUGHT WITH MY FISTS,"

"EVENTUALLY I SOUGHT ESCAPE FROM TORMENT IN SELF-DESTRUCTION..."

"THIS WAS MY BAPTISM OF SOLITUDE."

"FOR TWO YEARS I WAS A HERMIT... ALONE,"

"I WAS WAITING..."

LATER, AS I GREW MORE ACCUSTOMED TO MY POWER I BEGAN TO QUESTION ITS SOURCE. WAS IT SCIENCE, OR MAGIC?

"...BUT **EVERY-THING** THAT WAS HAPPENING TO ME WAS SO STRANGE, SO BIZARRE,"

"I DIVED FROM THE PLANE INTO THE OCEAN, BUT I DID NOT DIE..."

"NOT THEN."

"WAITING TO BE SHOWN..."

"...WAITING FOR THE CONJURER TO REVEAL HIS TRICKS."

"THE **BLACK KNIGHT** CAME AND SHOWED ME MYSTERIES OF MAGIC,"

"MERLIN NURTURED ME IN OTHERWORLD, FOR A TIME I WAS AT PEACE,"

"WE FOUGHT WITH WRAITHS AND SHADOWBEASTS AND WALKED WITH ANCIENT FEAR."

"HE HELPED ME INTO OTHERWORLD, INTO THE PRESENCE OF **MERLIN,** INTO THE PRESENCE OF INCARNATE LEGEND,"

"BUT THEN I HAD TO FIGHT AGAIN, TO SAVE A WORLD GONE **MAD.**"

41

42

43

STRANGE HOW FEW PEOPLE REMEMBER SIR JAMES JASPERS.

STILL... POLITICS IS LIKE THAT.

AS YOU KNOW, GENTLEMEN, CAPTAIN BRITAIN IS BACK IN ACTION.

FAMILY HOMELESS AFTER STAR WARS BATTLE

Mrs Joan Scott, and her family who were made homeless as the result of the extraordinary "Star Wars" battle which took place in their living room, yesterday accepted the keys of a new property on the much sought after Bellingham Estate.

The incident which left Mrs Joan Scott, her father-in-law and daughter, Josie, homeless, occurred when a group of costumed intruders attacked a man who was a guest at Mrs Scott's house.

In a special ceremony, on the steps of the town hall, councillor Robert Varney presented Mrs Scott with the keys to her new home. But Mr. Varney's opponents on the council have seen the move to rehouse the Scott family so quickly as an "example of cynical electioneering." Local council elections are due to take place in days' time.

CB FILE

ALREADY WE HAVE A TEENAGE BYSTANDER KILLED AND EXTENSIVE DAMAGE TO PUBLIC PROPERTY.

IRONICALLY, BRADDOCK HAS ALSO RETURNED, SUPPOSEDLY FROM A JET-SET WORLD TOUR.

HE IS MAKING HIMSELF A PUBLIC FIGURE BY REBUILDING BRADDOCK MANOR AND OPENING UP THE FARMLANDS. LOTS OF JOBS. LOTS OF MEDIA.

GENTLEMEN, IN THE ABSENCE OF S.T.R.I.K.E. OR ANY OTHER CONTAINMENT GROUP, I WANT AUTHORITY TO INVESTIGATE BRADDOCK MANOR AND INTERVIEW BRIAN BRADDOCK.

INNOCENT LIVES ARE AT RISK WHILST THIS BEING OPERATES UNCHECKED, AND...

IN THE MEANTIME YOU WILL TAKE NO FURTHER ACTION.

GOOD DAY!

THANK YOU FOR YOUR REPORT, CHIEF INSPECTOR. WE SHALL CONSIDER IT.

"OUR MR. THOMAS CAN CERTAINLY BE TEDIOUS AT TIMES..."

"STILL... HE IS A GOOD POLICEMAN."

"WE'LL FOWARD HIS REPORT TO RCX. THAT'S WHAT THE BUNCH THAT REPLACED S.T.R.I.K.E. ARE CALLING THEMSELVES, ISN'T IT ?"

"THEY'LL TAKE CARE OF IT."

HE WALKS TO CLEAR HIS HEAD.

SOMETHING ABOUT THE WORLD IS OUT OF PLACE.

SOMETHING STRANGE IS GOING TO HAPPEN...

...SOON!

Next: Law & Disorder

WHY DO WE HAVE TO WALK HOME?

THE TAXI DRIVER WANTED PAPER-POUNDS TO BRING US THIS WAY, WE DIDN'T HAVE ANY.

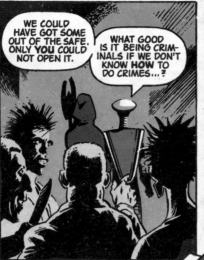

WE COULD HAVE GOT SOME OUT OF THE SAFE, ONLY YOU COULD NOT OPEN IT.

WHAT GOOD IS IT BEING CRIMINALS IF WE DON'T KNOW HOW TO DO CRIMES...?

AWRIGHT, YOU WEIRDOS, SHOW US SOME CASH! UNLESS YOU LIKE HOSPITAL FOOD, THAT IS...

WHAT STRANGE, RUDE CREATURES WE ARE AMONGST. THIS PLACE IS A PUZZLEMENT I DO NOT UNDERSTAND.

IF YOU ARE ROBBING US YOU HAVE MADE A MISTAKE—WE HAVE NOTHING...

...AND ANYWAY, WE ARE CRIMINALS TOO!

WHASS ISS THEN, IF YOU AIN'T GOT NOTHINK?

YUK HYUGGRRR

Captain BRITAIN

LAW & DISORDER

JAMIE DELANO & ALAN DAVIS
CO-CONSPIRATORS
AIDED AND ABETTED BY
STEVE CRADDOCK - LETTERER
CHRIS   GILL - EDITOR

ORF WIV ITS 'EAD!

DIDJA SEE THAT, SHIRL?

HE TRIED TO CUT MY 'EAD OFF WIV THAT AXE...

COR, DWAYNE, IT'S SMOOTH AS A BABY'S BUM!

...AND WE WOULDN'T HAVE TO LIVE IN THIS DISMAL PLACE IF WE COULD DO A PROPER CRIME.

IT'S ONLY A MATTER OF LEARNING THE ROPES, WE'RE BOUND TO MAKE MISTAKES AT FIRST...

WHAT WE NEED IS SOMEONE "CLEVER" TO TEACH US, TO SHOW US WHAT TO DO...

SHUT UP! YOU'RE STUPID! YOU GET ON MY NERVES!

46

I'M GOING OUTSIDE TO THINK ON MY OWN.

I DO LIKE THAT NICE JOHN WATT. NOT THAT NASTY MR. BARLOW, THOUGH, I AM GLAD THEY BROUGHT THIS BACK.

IT'S AN OLD CHINESE PROVERB, Y'KNOW, GLAD. 'SOFTLY SOFTLY CATCHEE MONKEY...'

THE PEOPLE TALKED IN RIDDLES, BUT THE PICTURE-BOX GAVE HIM IDEAS...

IT HAD SHOWN HIM THE WAY TO ROB THE SAFE, BUT SOMETHING HAD GONE WRONG.

HE WOULD WATCH MORE CLOSELY THIS TIME...

IT WAS EASY. THE PICTURE-BOX HAD SHOWN HIM EXACTLY HOW TO DO IT.

FIRST THEY HAD TO RAM THE VAN WITH A CAR...

NOW!

...THEN THEY HAD TO MAKE THE GUARDS OPEN THE BACK, WHERE THEY WOULD FIND THE SACKS OF PAPER-POUNDS.

WE'RE CRIMINALS. WE'RE ROBBING YOU.

WHAA?

IT WAS EASY...

47

...AS LONG AS EVERYONE PLAYED THE GAME.

GET LOST, CREEP. YOU'RE BARMY.

BUT YOU HAVE TO OPEN IT. WE'RE ROBBING YOU.

IT'S... IT'S THE RULES.

WHICH, OF COURSE, THEY DIDN'T.

HYUK YUK YUK YUK.

GET THE POUNDS! GET THE POUNDS!

YUK.

IT ALL WENT WRONG AGAIN.

IT'S ALL BURNT!

QUICK! RUN! HERE COME OLD BILL AND SWEENEY!

IT WASN'T LIKE THE PICTURE-BOX AT ALL.

OH YES? AND WHAT'S THE RCX THEN...

...THAT IT CAN STOP ME PURSUING CRIMINALS TO THE FULL EXTENT OF THE LAW?

YOU MAY CHECK OUR CREDENTIALS IF YOU WISH...

...BUT I ASSURE YOU THAT, AS REGULATORS, AGENT MICHAEL AND I HAVE COMPLETE AUTHORITY IN ALL MATTERS CONCERNING THE ACTIVITIES OF SUPERBEINGS...

RESOURCES CONTROL EXECUTIVE HAS ASSUMED THE FUNCTION OF THAT SOMEWHAT HEAVY-HANDED AGENCY, S.T.R.I.K.E.

AGENT GABRIEL AND MYSELF ARE PART OF A TEAM OF SPECIALISTS. WE ARE GHOST GUERILLAS, IF YOU LIKE. WE HAVE BEEN TRAINED TO FIGHT THESE MENACES.

WE HAVE LEARNED A GREAT DEAL SINCE THE DAYS OF S.T.R.I.K.E. — THE WORLD IS MUCH MORE FLUID NOW. WE HAVE SUBTLER METHODS, OUR STRATEGIES ARE OBLIQUE.

BUT WE MUST FUNCTION IN ISOLATION. THERE MUST BE NO INTERFERENCE FROM YOUR MEN, THOMAS.

WHAT WE NEED IS THE ONE WITH THE MOUSTACHE WHO BROUGHT US HERE...

WHERE DID HE BRING US FROM, THEN?

...FROM WHERE WE WERE.

HYUK.

IT WAS BETTER THERE, THE ONE WITH THE MOUSTACHE KNEW ALL THE THINGS TO DO. NOT LIKE YOU, YOU'RE USELESS.

HE'S DEAD THOUGH, ISN'T HE? HE BROUGHT US HERE AND DIED.

NOTHING MAKES SENSE HERE. WHY DID HE BRING US?

HE WAS A LEADER, THAT'S WHY.

A LEADER, THAT'S WHAT THEY'RE CALLED. WE NEED A LEADER.

I TOLD YOU SO.

BUT WHERE ARE WE GOING TO GET ONE?

THAT'S IT!

IT SAYS HERE WE CAN ADVERTISE AND REACH A POTENTIAL READERSHIP OF MANY THOUSANDS...

WHAT'S ADVERTISE?

...YES, YOU HAVE GOT IT RIGHT. YES... END IT WITH 'CONTACT THE CRAZY GANG,' AND THEN THE ADDRESS.

...NO, IT'S NOT A JOKE...

WHAT IS A JOKE?

IT'S FUNNY, THE DAFT THINGS PEOPLE PUT INTO THE PERSONAL ADS. LISTEN TO THIS. 'COME BACK PETER, ALL IS FORGIVEN. FLOPSY, MOPSY AND COTTONTAIL!'

THE MIND BOGGLES, DOESN'T IT? NO?

HERE'S A STRANGE ONE, LISTEN—

'KEEN CRIMINALS REQUIRE CLEVER LEADERS. CONTACT THE CRAZY GANG,' AND THEN AN ADDRESS IN LONDON.

LET ME SEE THAT.

SURELY IT COULDN'T BE THEM, THEY WOULD HAVE COLLAPSED ALONG WITH JASPERS...

...BUT IF IT ISN'T THEM, SOMEONE HAS A PECULIARLY WARPED SENSE OF HUMOUR.

MANY DIVERSE PEOPLE READ 'THE TIMES!'

AH! IT IS THEM. ALLAH IS BOUNTIFUL WITH FORTUNE. THIS IS A NIGHT OF GRACE.

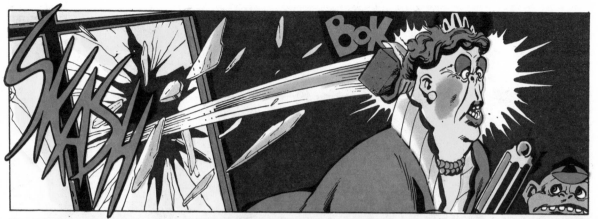

ORF WIV ITS 'EAD! ORF WIV ITS 'EAD!

YUK.

I AM a LEADER of extreme Genius I will SEND A car for You

HERE WE ARE, THEN...ER... CHAPS. THIS IS THE PLACE. FLAT 69 YOU WANT.

SEE, IT WORKED!

WE'RE GOING TO HAVE AN EXTREME GENIUS FOR A LEADER, WE'LL BE ALRIGHT NOW...

WE'RE CRIMINALS, YOU KNOW. WE'RE GOING TO MEET OUR LEADER.

YEAH? WELL, I DON'T REALLY THINK I WANT TO KNOW THAT, DO I GUV-KNOW WHAT I MEAN?

TAT-TAR.

WE'VE COME TO SEE THE EXTREME GENIUS.

SPEAK

PRESS

ENTER...

52

TODAY'S RAID ON THE NATIONAL GALLERY, THE FOURTH IN THIS WEEK'S SPATE OF RUTHLESS, HIGHLY-ORGANISED ROBBERIES, NETTED PAINTINGS DESCRIBED BY EXPERTS AS 'PRICELESS'...

A SLOW, STRONG ANGER TURNED WITHIN HIM...

POLICE ARE SAID TO BE BAFFLED BY THE SUPERCRIMES. THESE HAVE INCLUDED A HAUL OF EGYPTIAN GOLD FROM THE BRITISH MUSEUM AND SEVERAL HUNDRED THOUSAND POUNDS FROM THE ROYAL MINT...

...AND GREW,

ONE EYEWITNESS CLAIMED THAT THE GANG WERE DISGUISED AS STORYBOOK CHARACTERS...

IT HAD TO BE THE CRAZY GANG. THIS ANARCHY HAD THEIR STAMP.

HOW DARE THEY CORRUPT HIS WORLD WITH THEIR MADNESS?

WHY HAD THEY NOT DISSOLVED WITH ALL THE OTHER FOUL CREATIONS OF THE JASPERS WARP?

WELL, MY STRANGE FRIENDS... ARE YOU HAPPY WITH THE WEEK'S HAUL? SUCH TREASURE, EH? SUCH RICHES.

THEY WERE AN ANOMALY WHICH HE MUST ERADICATE.

YES, IT IS A MARVEL. IT IS GOOD TO HAVE A LEADER WHO IS LIKE US, AND ALSO AN EXTREME GENIUS.

THANK YOU.

WAIT! SILENCE! I HAVE BEEN DISOBEYED. ONE OF YOU IS MISSING—WHERE IS THE SMALL, DISGUSTING ONE?

I EXPRESSLY FORBADE ANY OF YOU TO LEAVE HERE WITHOUT MY PERMISSION...

CRAZY GANG REZIDUNC

COND KEE OU

HIS ANGER FOLLOWED HIM DOWN INTO THE STREETS,

TO THE ADDRESS FROM THE ADVERTISEMENT, THE ONLY LEAD HE HAD.

WE ARE VERY HUMBLE AND SORRY, EXTREME GENIUS.

"...HE WENT TO PLAY WITH HIS RATS."

HYUK—

CRAZY GANG REZIDUNC

CONDEMNED KEEP

C'MON, YOU LITTLE **MONSTER**, TAKE ME TO THE REST OF YOUR CRIMINAL CRONIES...

THRAK'

AH! CAPTAIN BRITAIN! SOONER THAN EXPECTED, BUT EXPECTED NONETHELESS.

YOU WILL, OF COURSE, CONSIDER YOURSELF MY PRISONER, YOU ARE HOPELESSLY OUTNUMBERED.

PRISONER! DON'T BE RIDICULAAAARRG

HYOCHOMP!

54

"CAPTURE HIM, DON'T KILL HIM."

CAREFULLY, DO NOT DAMAGE OUR FRIEND, WE HAVE MUCH TO TALK ABOUT...

IN THAT CASE, PERHAPS IT IS TIME TO PERFORM MY SMALL METAMORPHOSIS.

SLAYMASTER! YOU'RE FREE!

AS A BIRD, CAPTAIN. AS A BIRD.

WHEREAS YOU, I'M AFRAID, ARE NOT.

I AM NO "FRIEND" TO CRIMINALS, AND NEITHER AM I IN THE HABIT OF TALKING TO "CATERPILLARS."

Next: **Flotsam & Jetsam**

YOU SURE YOU'RE ALRIGHT WITH THAT, MATE? YOU DON'T WANT TO DO YOURSELF AN INJURY...

YES. THANK YOU FOR YOUR HELP. YOU WILL, OF COURSE, FORGET WHERE IT WAS YOU BROUGHT ME, SHOULD YOU EVER BE ASKED...

SECRETS.

A SECRET ENTRANCE ...A SECRET BURDEN.

A SECRET PURPOSE...

...AT A SECRET DESTINATION.

SLAYMASTER, HELLO. WHAT BRINGS YOU SNIFFING ROUND MY BACK DOOR? COME TO WISH ME HAPPY BIRTHDAY?

YOUR BIRTH-DAY? THIS IS MOST AUSPICIOUS! I HAVE CHOSEN MY DAY WELL. PLEASE ACCEPT MY HUMBLE OFFERING...

Captain BRITAIN

Flotsam and Jetsam

WITH MY COMPLIMENTS, MADAM VIXEN...

...FOR YOU.

JAMIE DELANO
ALAN DAVIS
CO-CREATORS
S.CRADDOCK
LETTERER
IAN RIMMER
EDITOR

"HE FOUGHT BRAVELY, AS YOU WOULD EXPECT, BUT BLINDLY."

"...DIVINELY."

WHO'S A CLEVER BOY, THEN? AND TELL ME, WHERE ARE THE CRAZY GANG NOW?

"HIS RAGE WAS FEARSOME TO BEHOLD."

"BUT IT WAS ALL IN VAIN, FOR HE WAS OUTMATCHED..."

THEY HAD SERVED THEIR PURPOSE. I HAD NO MORE USE FOR THEM. I LET THEM GO.

HE'S NOT REALLY ONE OF US. HE TRICKED US.

WE'LL GO NOW. COME ON.

Hmmm. NOT VERY CLEVER, LEAVING THEM LOOSE LIKE THAT...

STILL, NEVER MIND. IT LOOKS AS IF MY GIFT HAS WOKEN UP IN A BIT OF A PADDY. PERHAPS I'D BETTER GO AND CALM HIM DOWN.

WHAT ARE YOU GOING TO DO WITH HIM? WHERE IS HIS COSTUME, VIXEN?

YOU CAN HAVE THE MAN, BUT I WANT HIS COSTUME.

WHAT MAKES YOU THINK THAT YOU'RE IN A POSITION TO WANT ANYTHING, CHAPPIE?

I BROUGHT HIM TO YOU! I THOUGHT WE WOULD COLLABORATE... USE HIM. I AM NOT ONE OF YOUR SERVING BOYS...

YOU ARE PRECISELY WHAT I SAY YOU ARE... CHAPPIE.

JOOLS! SIMON!

DEAR SLAYMASTER... DID YOU REALLY THINK I WOULD LET YOU HAVE THE COSTUME... HOW SWEET.

NO... YOU ARE FAR TOO DANGEROUS ALREADY. I'LL LET MY EGGHEADS FIND OUT HOW IT WORKS. THEN, PERHAPS, I SHALL HAVE ONE LIKE IT. I DO LIKE DRESSING UP.

I'LL LEAVE YOU NOW AND HAVE A CLOSER LOOK AT MY NEW TOY. THE BOYS WILL LOOK AFTER YOU...

WATCH IF YOU WANT... TA-TA.

I'LL KILL YOU FOR THIS, VIXEN! YOU'VE MADE A REASON TO FEAR ME.

CAPTAIN, CAPTAIN... SUCH HELPLESS POWER IS ENTERTAINING, I'LL EVEN CONFESS TO A SLIGHT FLUTTER OF THE HEART...

...BUT FEAR? NO, YOU DO NOT FRIGHTEN ME, YOU ARE PATHETIC.

NEVER THREATEN ME AGAIN.

YOU ARE MINE NOW, "HERO"... TO DO WITH AS I PLEASE!

WHAT DO YOU WANT WITH ME?

COME DOWN HERE... AND I'LL WHISPER TO YOU...

DISGUST AND A COLD, HARD ANGER FILL HIM. THIS IS NOT AN HONOURABLE WAY TO TREAT A WORTHY FOE...

...AND ANYWAY, HE WANTS THE COSTUME.

HE MOVES.

HE IS FAST. VERY FAST.

HE SHOULD HAVE KNOWN BETTER THAN TO TRUST HER. THE VIXEN DOES NOT SHARE HIS CODE OF ETHICS...

...SHE IS SHREWD AND VICIOUS, BUT HE IS A MATCH FOR HER. HE WILL FIND THE LABORATORY AND RECOVER THE COSTUME...

THEN HE WILL REDRESS THE BALANCE.

WELL, MY LITTLE BAND OF GLITTERING SOCIALITES, WE ARE NO LONGER RESTING. WE HAVE A JOB...

Er... Mother...

...YES, IT'S PARTYTIME AGAIN. YOUNG BONE-BAG HERE HAS FIXED HIS NASTY LITTLE BRAIN ONTO THE TARGET. WE HAVE THE KONTRACT, WE'RE READY TO ROLL...

Sorry Mother, but we're not. I've er... lost the er... fix.

WHAT DO YOU MEAN, YOU'VE LOST THE FIX? WE NEED THOSE CO-ORDINATES...

...AND STOP CALLING ME MOTHER, MY NAME IS GATE-CRASHER.

Sorry Mother, but it just... twinkled out. I'm trying to relocate.

HIS ANGER STILL BURNS. THE ARROGANCE OF THE WOMAN, BUT IF SHE DOES NOT WANT CO-OPERATION, THEN SHE MUST HAVE OPPOSITION.

HE WILL TEACH HER RESPECT.

LAB 4

THE INITIAL EXAMINATION OF THE ER... GARMENT SHOWS THAT IT IS, MORE PROPERLY, A MACHINE...

CAN THIS EMPTY GARMENT BE THE SOURCE OF HIS OLD ENEMY'S POWER..?

IT LOOKS EMPTY. IT NEEDS A BODY TO FILL IT. IT NEEDS COURAGE.

... BUT THE MICROCIRCUITRY IS INCREDIBLY COMPLEX. I DON'T KNOW IF THE COMPUTER CAN COMPLETELY ANALYSE IT.

THE COSTUME MOULDS TO HIM LIKE A NEW SKIN.

WILD EXCITEMENT FLEXES WITHIN HIM. HE WANTS TO LAUGH.

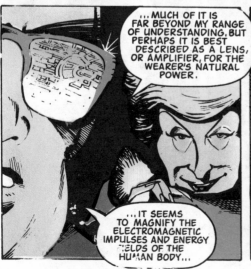

... MUCH OF IT IS FAR BEYOND MY RANGE OF UNDERSTANDING, BUT PERHAPS IT IS BEST DESCRIBED AS A LENS, OR AMPLIFIER, FOR THE WEARER'S NATURAL POWER.

... IT SEEMS TO MAGNIFY THE ELECTROMAGNETIC IMPULSES AND ENERGY FIELDS OF THE HUMAN BODY...

HE FEELS THE POWER — A MAN OF IRON IN A BALSA WOOD WORLD.

HE PLAYS WITH HIS NEW STRENGTH, TESTING.

MAGNIFICENT. HIS CONTROL IS PERFECT.

...IT CREATES A PERSONAL FORCEFIELD...

...AND CAN NEGATE OR DIRECT GRAVITY, GIVING THE POWER OF FLIGHT...

IMMENSELY STRONG, YES— BUT HE IS NOT INVULNERABLE.

THERE IS STILL PAIN.

MATHEMATICAL PROJECTIONS SHOW ENORMOUS POTENTIAL POWER...

LAB 4

HE IS IRON, BUT HE SHOULD BE DIAMOND.

THERE ARE MORE SECRETS TO BE LEARNED...

WAKE UP, CAPTAIN. WHERE IS THE VIXEN?

GONE... I DON'T KNOW...

PLEASE BELIEVE ME WHEN I SAY THAT IT WAS NEVER MY INTENTION TO SEE YOU THUS HUMILIATED.

WE HAVE LONG BEEN ENEMIES, AND I WOULD HAVE PREFERRED MY FINAL VICTORY TO HAVE CARRIED MORE HONOUR...

...BUT DEFEATED YOU ARE. UTTERLY. AND I MUST KNOW THE SECRETS OF THIS SUIT. YOU HAVE LOST, CAPTAIN, SO TELL ME... QUICKLY.

YOU NEED TO WEAR THE HELMET...

IT'S TOO LATE FOR EXCUSES, THE DAMAGE IS ALREADY DONE... YOU— TELL ME, WHAT CAN SLAYMASTER DO WITH THIS COSTUME?

WELL, THE KEY TO IT ALL WOULD SEEM TO BE THE HELMET...

YOU LIE, CAPTAIN, I FEEL NO DIFFERENCE...

"...WITHOUT THE HELMET, THE SUIT ACTS IN A PURELY MECHANICAL FASHION. IT AMPLIFIES THE USER'S STRENGTH CONSIDERABLY, BUT THAT IS ALL."

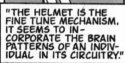

"THE HELMET IS THE FINE TUNE MECHANISM. IT SEEMS TO IN-CORPORATE THE BRAIN PATTERNS OF AN INDIV-IDUAL IN ITS CIRCUITRY."

"WHEN COMBINED WITH THE COSTUME, IT MUST HAVE THE POTENTIAL TO EXTEND ALL THE FUNCTIONS OF THE USER TO THE SUPERHUMAN CATEGORY..."

"HOWEVER, BECAUSE IT IS MATCHED SO PERFECTLY TO ONE SPECIFIC BRAIN, I WOULD IMAGINE THAT FOR A USER WITH A DIFFERENT BRAIN PATT-ERN THERE WOULD BE LITTLE ADVANTAGE..."

"...MAYBE EVEN ACTUAL HARM."

63

I CAN'T BELIEVE YOU'RE DOING THIS! YOU'RE CONTROLLING THE SUIT WITH YOUR MIND...

YES, I THINK I MUST BE. WHAT WAS IT YOU WERE SAYING ABOUT DEFEAT AND HUMILIATION...?

YOU CAN FLY IN THAT SUIT, YOU KNOW...

SO FLY.

I DON'T LIKE PEOPLE WEARING MY CLOTHES...

I DON'T LIKE BEING KEPT PRISONER...

...AND I DON'T LIKE BEING WATCHED WHILE I'M DRESSING!

HEAR THIS, VIXEN. I'M GOING TO TAKE THIS PLACE APART BRICK BY BRICK UNTIL I FIND YOU...

...AND WHEN I DO, I'M GOING TO...

OH DEAR, HE IS RATHER CROSS, ISN'T HE? I REALLY THINK HE MEANS IT. I THINK WE OUGHT TO CUT OUR LOSSES ON THIS ONE...

PETER, VIVIAN, WILL YOU BE ANGELS AND GO AND FLUSH THE CELLS? QUICK AS YOU CAN NOW, DEARS...

...THERE'S NOWHERE I WON'T FIND...

OH NO!

HE GULPS A LAST MOUTHFUL OF AIR BEFORE THE ROARING BLACKNESS SWALLOWS HIM.

THERE IS A BREATHLESS ETERNITY OF SOUND AND MOVEMENT...

...THEN, MERCIFULLY, AN ANCHOR. HE GRATEFULLY CLIMBS TOWARDS THE LIGHT.

WHAT IN GOD'S NAME...?

EXHAUSTED AND HALF-DROWNED, FOR A SECOND HE CONSIDERS DUCKING BACK DOWN AND CLOSING THE LID ABOVE HIM. BUT HE IS A HERO...

AND THIS IS HERO'S BUSINESS.

Next: Sid's Story

ITCHY SKIN, INFLAMED AND PEELING.

MOULDERING SCABS, DECAYING, DRIBBLING.

THAT WAS HOW IT STARTED.

THEN BOUQUETS OF ANGRY BOILS SWELLED TENDER, RED AND RIPE.

AND BILIOUS SLIME, DIMLY AMBER CURDLED IN JAUNDICED WOUNDS.

RIVERS OF PUTRID PHLEGM CASCADED FROM SCARLET SORES AS FRACTURED BONE RUPTURED ROTTING FLESH.

CRIMSON AGONY SOAKED INTO TATTERED CLOTHING. SULLIED BODY AND SOILED GARMENT TWISTED AND MERGED... A SWIRLING MOSAIC OF FUSED FLESH AND FABRIC.

THAT WAS HOW IT CONTINUED.

Captain BRITAIN

SIDNEY CRUMB IS ILL.

"I DON'T FEEL GOOD. AIN'T DONE FOR WEEKS."

"I NEED 'ELP. SOMETHING MEDICINAL. GET ME BACK ON ME FEET. BE OKAY THEN."

MIKE COLLINS
ALAN DAVIS
CO-CREATORS
ANNIE HALFACREE
LETTERER
IAN RIMMER
EDITOR

SIDS STORY

THROUGH A HAZE OF PAIN AND ALCOHOL HE NOTICES MOVEMENT IN THE RAIN.

"LOOK AT THEM KIDS—BLIGHTERS OUGHTER BE AT SCHOOL!"

"AIN'T NO DISCIPLINE... ALL OF 'EM, TOO CHEEKY..."

TIME ALTERS. MEMORIES AND REALITY BLEED INTO EACH OTHER...

CHEEK ME WOULD YOU?

THIS'LL TEACH YER, YER LITTLE BEGGAR!

MEMORIES OF WANTON VIOLENCE FROM A DRUNKEN FATHER...

"MEBBE THEM KIDS CAN 'ELP. IF'N THEY AIN'T SNIFFERS, THAT IS..."

"UHH—HURTS JUST TO STAND UP..."

AY! AY, STEVE! 'IM OVER THERE, LOOK AT 'IM!

WO'? JUST A GRUBBY TRAMP INNIT? FORGET 'IM— JUST BE CADGIN' FER MONEY!

IT AIN'T A TRAMP, NIGE—

—IT AIN'T!!!

AND FOR SID, TIME ALTERS AGAIN...

...AIN'T YOUR LUCKY DAY CRUMBIE!!

NAH, NOT MEETIN' US, IT AIN'T!

...INTO SCHOOL DAYS IN THE WAR—THE WAR WHICH STOLE AWAY A SODDEN FATHER AND LEFT HIM WITH A MOTHER WHO COULDN'T PROVIDE ENOUGH...

YOU'RE A MESS, CRUMBIE, YOU BELONG IN THE DIRT!

HAH HAH! GETTIM, GEORGE!

BUT IN THE DREAM THERE IS INTRUSION... OUT ON THE PERIPHERY... IT'S INDEFINABLE, THEN IT'S GONE.

"THEM BULLIES — NOT FAIR..."

"NEVER FAIR."

AND HE SHAMBLES ON, OBLIVIOUS.

COME ON, YOU SCRAWNY REPTILE... TRY HARDER. WE CAN'T HOVER HERE FOR LONG, AND I WANT A DEFINITE FIX BEFORE WE CORPORATE...

I'm sorry Mother...don't be cross. The field is blank, I can't...

No! Wait... Something flashed... Yes, he's there... underground... moving fast... dodging...

LOCK ON, LOCK ON... TRACK HIM. IF YOU LOSE HIM I'M GOING TO SQUASH YOU.

I got him Mother...I got him. Tight fix... tight fix...he's fast and weaving...

OKAY. LET'S MOVE... STAY WITH HIM...

...AND STOP CALLING ME MOTHER.

'ERE, DOREEN--WOT'S 'APPENIN'?

BROWN

DUNNO JOYCE, THEM PEOPLE ALL LOOK PETRIFIED, I WONDER WHAT'S--

"--CAUSING IT..."

"NO ONE'LL STOP AND TALK TO ME! AIN'T FAIR THAT I DON'T GET NO RESPECT..."

"GET A BIT DOWN ON YER LUCK, AN' YER TREATED LIKE DIRT."

JEANZ

OH MY GOD!

AGGGH!

CONTROL, I'M AT A MAJOR DISTURBANCE AT THE ROTUNDA PRECINCT. REQUEST ASSISTANCE-- AND QUICK! OUT!

NOW LISTEN IN THERE... I'VE CALLED REINFORCEMENTS IN, SO YOU'D BETTER CALM DOWN AND--

BLOODY HELL!

"TROUBLE, ALWAYS TROUBLE... EVEN MAVIS..."

TIME ALTERS ONCE MORE. IT'S THE LAST DAY OF A DRINK-WRECKED MARRIAGE...

I'VE HAD ENOUGH! I CAN'T STAND ANOTHER DAY IN THIS HOVEL WATCHING YOU DRINK YOURSELF INTO THE GROUND!

SEE YOU AT YOUR FUNERAL, SID.

THE VAGUE INTRUSION CREEPS IN EVEN MORE, BUT PASSES WITH THE VISION...

"DAMN YOU, MAVIS!"

"YOU COULD HAVE STAYED!"

"MY JOB HAD GONE — YOU SHOULDN'T'VE TOO.!"

"YOU TOOK ALL MY RESPECT WITH YOU, MAVIS!"

"I'M ILL, MAVIS, I DON'T NEED THE HASSLE.!"

"I NEED... MEDICINE."

WE CAN'T CONTROL THE SITUATION! GET THE BLOODY ARMY IN!

71

SHE IS ROMA.

SHE IS ANXIOUS.

SHE INHERITED THE REINS OF THE MULTI-VERSE WHEN MERLIN, HER FATHER, DIED. A COMPLEX KNOWLEDGE FOR AN IMMORTAL SO YOUNG.

NOW JUST ONE EXISTENCE HOLDS HER OVERSEEING EYE. AN EXISTENCE THAT IS THE CAUSE OF HER ANXIETY.

CAN HE SURVIVE IT? HE HAS BORNE MUCH MORE THAN HIS SHARE.

THE GUILT IS MINE. I BROUGHT THEM TOGETHER AT MY FATHER'S DYING. I SHOULD HAVE FORSEEN IT.

"I WATCHED THE ROGUE STUDYING HIM AND PLOTTING. I DID NOT WANT TO MEDDLE. THAT WAS MY FATHER'S WAY."

"THE ONSLAUGHT BEGAN AND STILL I ONLY WATCHED."

I LEFT IT TO HIS SISTER'S FLEDGLING POWER TO SHIELD HIM FROM DEATH. I DID NOT STRETCH OUT MY HAND.

EVERY INSTINCT IS TO HELP HIM...

BUT NO—I WILL NOT DO AS MY FATHER, AND INTERVENE. THE CAPTAIN MUST STRUGGLE ALONE.

73

"I KNOW HIM...IT'S THAT BIG PONCE! THE ONE WHO THINKS HE'S AN 'ERO! *HE'LL* HELP ME—HE'S *GOT* TOO!"

AND TIME ALTERS. REALITY SHIFTS AND BLEEDS ONE FINAL TIME, TO THE RUBBISH TIP WHERE HIS LAST FRIEND HAS VANISHED...

MRS. McGEARY? WAS THAT YOU SAYING 'SHIZIK' JUST THEN?

MRS. McGEARY?

AIN'T YOUR LUCKY DAY!

LITTLE BEGGAR!

SEE YOU AT YOUR FUNERAL, SID!

THE FACES OF THE PAST SHIFT AND GEL, AND THE ANOMALY RETURNS, NO LONGER AT THE EDGE OF HIS VISION...

...BUT AT ITS *CENTRE.*

IT IS THE *FURY.* IT IS THE SUPREME KILLING MACHINE. IT HAS CROSSED THE PARALLEL REALITIES TO HUNT ITS PREY, *CAPTAIN BRITAIN.*

BUT IT HAS PAID *HEAVILY* FOR ITS VIOLATION OF REALITIES. STUNTED AND DAMAGED BY ITS FLIGHT, IT NEEDS *MATTER* TO REBUILD ITSELF...

SHI— ZIK—

WITH MRS. McGEARY, IT WAS DEADLY ACCURATE.

SUCH GOOD FORTUNE COULD NEVER BE SID'S...

WITH THE WOUND COMES INFECTION.

THE FURY'S POWER OF MUTATION HAS BECOME SIDNEY CRUMB'S *CURSE.*

"THAT *THING* DID IT! I CAN'T BE CURED!"

"STOP IT! STOP IT!"

"PLEASE STOP HURTING ME!"

I CAN'T LET IT GET AWAY. I'VE GOT TO DESTROY IT—BEFORE IT BECOMES MORE POWERFUL...

PLEASE STOP HURTING ME

IT SCREAMED! IT SCREAMED! I HEARD—NO, FELT IT... IT ISN'T MALEVOLENT, IT'S IN PAIN...

"...AIN'T FAIR..."

...DYING.

"OUGHTER BE MORE...RESPECT..."

"...WHEN A BLOKE'S GOIN' TO —"

THAT'S SORTED THAT OUT THEN...

WHAT...?

YOU DID IT, CAPTAIN. YOU JUST SMEARED IT INTO THE PAVEMENT. WE WON!

DID WE?

NOT LEGION, KAPTAIN.... NOT ME. THAT'S ANOTHER BROTHER.

...AND FASCINATION? SHE'S **OUR** FRIEND NOW... THERE **IS** NO SPECIAL EXECUTIVE... NOT YET...

WAR DOG WON'T EVEN BE WHELPED FOR ANOTHER HUNDRED YEARS. AND COBWEB IS ELSEWHERE. **WE** ARE A **FAR** MORE SENIOR ELITE...

FASCINATION....? LEGION....? WHY.....? WHAT DOES THE SPECIAL EXECUTIVE WANT WITH ME NOW..?

...GATECRASHER'S TECHNET.

KAPTAIN BRITON, YOU HAVE THE HONOUR TO BE OUR PRISONER.

Next: **Double Game**

Captain BRITAIN

DOUBLE GAME

THE AIR SCREAMS LIKE SIRENS AROUND HIM.

THERE ARE ENEMIES IN HIS CAMP.

JAMIE DELANO
ALAN DAVIS
CO-CREATORS
ANNIE HALFACREE
LETTERER
IAN RIMMER
EDITOR

HE SHOULD BE AT HOME.

HIS FAMILY IS THREATENED.

WHAT'S THE MATTER, BRIAN? YOU LOOK...

STRANGE.

FOR A FRAGMENTED MOMENT IT IS LIKE FLYING INTO A MIRROR...

FOR A SECOND HE ALMOST CAN'T DO IT...

...CAN'T FACE HIMSELF.

BUT THEN THE ANGER TAKES OVER... AND IT IS JUST FIGHTING AGAIN.

SKASH

BUT PERHAPS IN THE COURSE OF OUR RATHER HECTIC ARRIVAL I **HAVE** NEGLECTED THE NICETIES OF SOCIAL CONVENTION...

GATHER ROUND, CHILDREN, AND WHILE THE WARRIORS STRIVE ON, I WILL TRY TO SET YOUR ANXIOUS MINDS AT REST.

MY NAME IS GATECRASHER. THESE ARE THE TECHNET. WE HAVE COME TO YOUR TIMEZONE IN PURSUIT OF A RUTHLESS FUGITIVE, A THING WE DO FOR MONEY...

WHAT FUGITIVE? NOT BRIAN?

PATIENCE, PATIENCE. ALL WILL BE REVEALED.

"IT SHOULD HAVE BEEN A BREEZE. WE HAD HIS IMPRINT, FIXED HIM COLD. BUT HE HAD SOME PRESSING BUSINESS. WE WAITED FOR OUR MOMENT... THEN..."

"THERE WAS A LOT OF ACTIVITY AROUND US. WE WERE ANXIOUS TO BE AWAY WITH OUR PRIZE. BUT SOMETHING ABOUT HIM CAUSED US DOUBT..."

He knows Legion and the Special Executive, but not us. That does not match the target's record.

"THE SNATCH WAS RIPE. IT **WAS** A TIGHT FIX. WE PULLED HIM FROM THE AIR LIKE FRUIT."

Snared, snared... Pull him down, Mother. It's a clear match on the scan. I found him, Mother — I said I would.

"IT DID NOT TAKE LONG TO ESTABLISH THAT THE ELECTRONIC AURA OF THE BEING'S SUIT HAD BEEN ALTERED TO MATCH THAT OF THE TARGET."

YOU'VE BEEN PULLED BY A DECOY, YOU WORTHLESS, SCRAWNY LIZARD!

"WE WERE UNDER OBSERVATION. APOLOGIES WERE BRIEF BUT SINCERE..."

SCAN WIDE. AND THIS TIME **FIND** HIM... OR I'LL HAVE YOUR ARMS FOR TOOTHPICKS!

SORRY, CAPTAIN.

AHEM.

"HE WAS CUNNING, THIS KAPTAIN BRITON. HE HAD LURED US TO THIS UNIVERSE AND CROSSED TRAILS WITH HIS 'PARAFORM', CAPTAIN BRITAIN.

I have something, Mother. It **has** to be...

...Yes. I'm certain... North North-West... not far.

CAPTAIN... **WAIT!** TOO LATE— SUCH AN IMPULSIVE CREATURE.

GATECRASHER... LOOK!

SO THIS IMPOSTER IS PRETENDING TO BE ME..?

"THE CAPTAIN GRASPED THE CONCEPT IMMEDIATELY..."

NORTH NORTH-WEST..? BETSY!

"THE PARTY WAS GETTING TOO CROWDED. WE DID NOT HAVE TIME TO BE SOCIABLE. WE FOLLOWED..."

LOCK ON, BONEBAG... LOCK ON. WE MOVE.

ALIEN LIFE FORMS DISCORPORATING... EIGHT, NO NINE. THE SUPERHUMAN IS AIRBORNE, TRACK NORTH NORTH-WEST. MACH... HE'S VERY FAST.

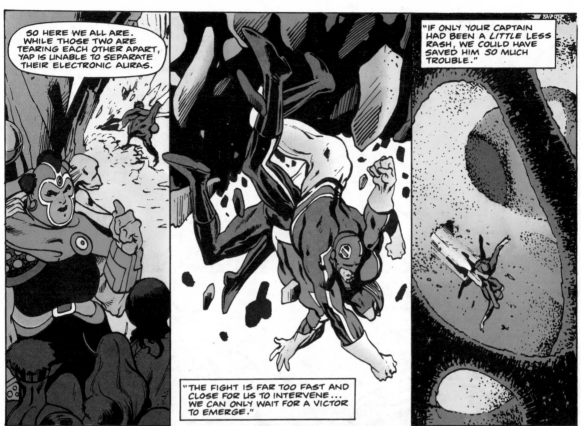

SO HERE WE ALL ARE. WHILE THOSE TWO ARE TEARING EACH OTHER APART, YAP IS UNABLE TO SEPARATE THEIR ELECTRONIC AURAS.

"IF ONLY YOUR CAPTAIN HAD BEEN A *LITTLE* LESS RASH, WE COULD HAVE SAVED HIM *SO MUCH* TROUBLE."

"THE FIGHT IS FAR TOO FAST AND CLOSE FOR US TO INTERVENE... WE CAN ONLY WAIT FOR A VICTOR TO EMERGE."

SPECIAL RESPONSIBILITIES FOR SUPERBEINGS, EH? WHAT DO YOU DO — SWEEP UP AFTER THEM?

I'VE TOLD YOU WHO IS RESPONSIBLE. AND IF *YOU* WON'T DO ANYTHING ABOUT BRADDOCK, I *WILL*!

HE IS BORING, ISN'T HE?

INSPECTOR! I THINK THAT YOU HAVE FAILED TO GRASP THAT WE HAVE *ABSOLUTE* CONTROL...

YOU CAN'T HIT ME AND GET AWAY WITH IT... I'M A POLICE...

OFFICER, UNDERSTAND THIS. IF I WANT *YOU* TO DISAPPEAR, YOU *WILL* DISAPPEAR.

FROM THE SUDDEN SILENCE, IT WOULD SEEM THAT THE FIGHTING IS DONE. SHALL WE PREPARE TO GREET THE VICTOR?

YOU, CHICKEN, STAND BY ME.

PARADOK, BE READY TO JUMP IF IT GETS OUT OF HAND... ELMO AND FASCINATION, WATCH THE OTHERS.

BRIAN?

CAPTAIN?

YES, IT'S ME.

HERE'S YOUR FUGITIVE. DO WHAT YOU LIKE WITH HIM—JUST GET HIM OUT OF MY SIGHT.

JUST A MOMENT!

YAP, MAKE NO MISTAKE—IS HE TELLING THE TRUTH?

The electron patterns coincide perfectly, Mother. This is the one we caught earlier.

AND YOU? IS THIS YOUR BROTHER? SCAN HIM. BE SURE.

'COURSE IT'S HIM. HE WON, DIDN'T HE? THE CAPTAIN ALWAYS WINS.

I...I CAN'T... MY HEAD'S FULL OF COTTON WOOL...

YOU, GIRL... THE OTHER TELEPATH... IS THIS CAPTAIN BRITAIN?

YES, YES IT IS. THANK GOD YOU'RE ALRIGHT, BRIAN. THE FIGHTING WAS SO TERRIBLE.

NEVER MIND. IT'S ALL OVER NOW.

ALRIGHT, MY HAPPY TROUPE, HOLD ON TO HIM NOW. PERHAPS WE SHOULD LABEL HIM... JUST IN CASE.

AND HOW ABOUT YOU, CHICKEN? SURE YOU WON'T COME ALONG FOR THE RIDE..?

Snee snee.

NO THANK YOU!

SUIT YOURSELF— BUT YOU DON'T KNOW WHAT YOU'RE MISSING.

THAT'S THE LAST WE'LL SEE OF HIM. PRETENDING TO BE ME... WHAT A NERVE.

WOW!

YOU SORTED HIM OUT THOUGH, DIDN'T YOU, CAPTAIN?

BRIAN, I'M EXHAUSTED. THAT THING WITH TENTACLES DID SOMETHING TO MY BRAIN. I'M NUMB.

I'LL SEE YOU TO YOUR ROOM.

I 'AVEN'T SEEN SO MUCH DAMAGE SINCE THE LAND-MINE HIT THE PLUME OF FEATHERS IN THE BLITZ...

NEVER MIND, WE'LL START THE CLEAR-UP IN THE MORNING.

OH DEAR. WE DID MAKE RATHER A MESS OF THE OLD PLACE, DIDN'T WE?

G'NIGHT, BRIAN... G'NIGHT, BETSY.

GOODNIGHT, MEGGAN.

I DID **TRY** TO HELP YOU, BRIAN. BUT THEY WOULDN'T LET ME...

I DID TRY.

I'M SORRY TO BE SO HELPLESS, BUT WILL YOU STAY UNTIL I'M ASLEEP? THAT DAMN CREATURE'S BLANKED ME OUT AND I FEEL A BIT VULNERABLE.

OF COURSE... DON'T WORRY, IT WILL PASS.

Panel 1: I'M GLAD YOU'RE BACK, BRIAN. I KNOW YOU HAVE A LOT OF THINGS TO DO, BUT SOMETIMES WE NEED YOU HERE.

I'LL STAY AS LONG AS YOU LIKE.

Panel 2: AFTER ALL, YOU ARE THE MASTER OF THE HOUSE.

YES... YES I AM, AREN'T I?

Panel 3: HE IS WARM.

SHE FEELS SECURE.

Panel 4: HE IS HER BROTHER.

BRI-MMM!

Panel 5: NO!

Panel 6: "NOOOOO..."

Next: **A Long Way From Home**

BEFORE HE OPENS HIS EYES HE KNOWS THAT HE IS NOT WHERE HE SHOULD BE.

HE SWEEPS THE CURTAINS OF PERFUMED SLEEP FROM HIS MIND AND MEMORY ILLUMINATES HIM.

HE HAD LOST THE FIGHT AT THE MANOR. HIS DOUBLE HAD BEATEN HIM.

CONFUSION SENDS RIPPLES OF NAUSEA THROUGH HIM. WHERE IS THIS PLACE THAT THEY HAVE BROUGHT HIM TO?

THE AIR IS NOT LIKE THE AIR OF EARTH. IT SMELLS OF HOT BRASS.

Captain BRITAIN

HE IS A LONG WAY FROM ENGLAND...

A LONG WAY FROM HOME

JAMIE DELANO
ALAN DAVIS
CO-CREATORS
ANNIE HALFACREE
LETTERER
IAN RIMMER
EDITOR

BETSY?

SATURNYNE!

HELLO.

IT WAS CRUEL OF YOU TO GO...

DID YOU REALLY THINK I WOULD EVER LET YOU LEAVE ME..?

WHAT... I DON'T...

...NO, MY KAPTAIN, I WANT YOU HERE...

...UNDERSTAND. I'VE NEVER...

...NOT RUNNING AROUND ON SOME INFERIOR WORLD, CHASING AFTER 'BETSYS'.

BUT BETSY IS MY SISTER...

SSHHH. STOP TALKING NOW...

COME HERE... SISTER.

W-WHY ARE YOU DOING THIS..?

FINEDAY TO YOU, SIR. HERE IS FIRSTFOOD.

HMMM... FIRSTFOOD..? WHAT..?

WHERE— WHERE IS SATURNYNE?

THE MASTREX, OPUL LUN SAT-YR-NIN, IS IN THE CHAMBER OF THE WORLD, ATTENDING TO THE BUSINESS OF THE EMPIRE. YOU ARE TO JOIN HER IN THE DROME WHEN YOU ARE DRESSED.

THERE ARE TO BE GREAT CELEBRATIONS AND KOMBATS!

CELEBRATIONS..?

BUT I MUST LEAVE...

LEAVE..? OH NO, SIR. THAT IS NOT THE MASTREX WISH. THE CELEBRATIONS HONOUR YOUR RETURN. THERE WILL BE MANY DEATHS TO YOUR GLORY!

SEE—I HAVE BROUGHT YOUR ROBES AND INSIGNIA!

THESE ARE NOT MY CLOTHES... I SHOULD BE SOMEWHERE ELSE. WHY AM I HERE?

WHY?

HEY. **HEY, YOU!**

...I KNOW THAT DRAGON-SCALES ARE NOT THE MOST CONVENIENT FORM OF PAYMENT, BUT, ON THE WERE-WORLDS — WHERE WE STAGE OUR NEXT LITTLE SHOW — THEY ARE IN GREAT DEMAND. SO STOP MOANING AND...

UH-OH.

WAIT! I WANT TO TALK TO YOU.

BUT DON'T YOU *SEE?* THE **IMPOSTER** BEAT *ME* IN THE FIGHT. HE TRICKED YOU **AGAIN.** DAMN YOU — YOU **MUST** GET ME BACK! HE'S *THERE...* IN MY HOUSE... WITH MY *SISTER!*

PLEASE STEP BACK. YOUR PROXIMITY IS OFFENSIVE.

TWO QUESTIONS. WHAT WERE THE FIRST WORDS I EVER SPOKE TO YOU? AND, IF WE TAKE YOU BACK, CAN YOU PAY US?

COME, COME, KAPTAIN. NO HARD FEELINGS, PLEASE. NO SOUR GRAPES. IT WAS BUT A JOB. WE DID IT FOR MONEY...

AS I REMEMBER, YOU TOLD ME THAT I SHOULD BE *HONOURED* TO BE YOUR PRISONER. AND WHY SHOULD I PAY WHEN *YOU'RE* AT FAULT?

BE THAT AS IT MAY, THERE ARE COSTS TO BE MET. TRAVEL ALONE IS EXPENSIVE. AND, SADLY, IT LOOKS AS IF THERE IS TO BE VIOLENCE AS WELL.

YOU FILTH...

YOU VILE...

DISGUSTING...

FILTH!

MY GOD.

IMPRESSIVE, EH?

WHAT IS IT? WHAT'S IT DONE TO THEM?

IT'S PANDORA... SENTIENT SLIME-MOULD. PRIMITIVE BUT VERY TOUGH... INCREDIBLE ELASTICITY. SUCKS THE LIFE OUT OF 'EM.

Ahhhhh... She's resting... She's full...very warm. Very sweet... soft...soft... soft...

RIGHT. ALL HANDS TO THE PUMPS. LET'S GET HER CLEARED UP.

MAKE SURE YOU'VE DISENGAGED, BONE-BAG. I DON'T WANT YOU GETTING SUCKED UP AND GOING CLAUSTRO ON ME.

HEY, LITTLE LIZARD... C'MON, SNAP OUT OF IT. IT'S OVER...C'MON NOW, LET HER GO...

"...IT'S OVER."

99

TIME PASSES. THE ONLY SOUND IS THE SUCKING OF THE PUMPS AS THE STOLEN LIFE OF THE CITY IS SWALLOWED AND SQUEEZED INTO TIGHT, TIGHT DARKNESS

NO ONE HAS SPOKEN. IT IS AS IF WORDS COULD NOT PENETRATE THE DEAD AIR.

HSSSSSSST!

ONE FEELS THAT ONE SHOULD HAVE SOMETHING GLIB TO SAY IN TIMES OF HORROR...

SATURNYNE...

Careful, Mother... Something alive... Something unhappy.

COME, CAPTAIN. THERE IS NOTHING TO BE DONE HERE. THE PARTY'S GONE SOUR. WE MUST BE AWAY.

NO! BYRON! COME BACK! I WON'T LET YOU GO...BYRON PLEASE DON'T GO!

BUT WE CAN'T JUST...

YOU HAVE NO CHOICE, CAPTAIN. THIS IS NOT YOUR CONCERN. YOU HAVE YOUR PLACE.

COME BACK! YOU CAN'T GO AGAIN...NOT AGAIN...

HE TURNS HIS BACK AND WALKS AWAY. FROM THE CHAMBER OF THE WORLD HER WORDS PURSUE HIM LIKE FRANTIC BIRDS.

HE THINKS OF ENGLAND, OF BETSY. OF HOME, WHERE HE SHOULD BE...

BRIAN... WHERE ARE YOU?

Next: **Things Fall Apart**

100

IN THE VAST CAVERNS BELOW BRADDOCK MANOR IT SHIMMERS, THINKING.

THEIR MINDS ARE LOW AND SLOW. THEIR VISION LIMITED.

THEY DO NOT USE ME. THEY DO NOT LET ME GROW. THEIR ALLEGIANCE IS NOT FIXED.

ITS JEWELLED PRESENT IS HERE AND NOW IN ENGLAND. ITS MEMORY, A QUANTUM LEAP IN ONE DIRECTION; ITS FUTURE, IN ANOTHER.

THEY HAVE NO CONCEPTION OF THE INFINITY OF KNOWLEDGE AND COMPLEXITY OF CAUSE AND EFFECT OF WHICH I AM A PART.

THEY LOSE SIGHT OF THE PURPOSE. THEY ARE DISTRACTED. DISRUPTIVE FORCES GATHER ROUND. CHAOS GNAWS AT THEM; WEAKENS THEM.

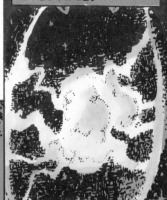

THINGS FALL APART

I WILL SEND MY EMISSARY TO TUTOR THEIR HAPHAZARD MINDS.

IT BECOMES NECESSARY THAT I TAKE CONTROL.

Captain BRITAIN

JAMIE DELANO   ALAN DAVIS
CO-CREATORS

ANNIE HALFACREE   IAN RIMMER
LETTERER   EDITOR

THE TECHNET HAVE ASSURED HIM THAT HE WILL RETURN TO BRADDOCK MANOR LESS THAN ONE EARTH HOUR AFTER HE LEFT...

ALISON, I CAN'T FIND BRIAN.

OH, MEGGAN! SOMETHING TERRIBLE HAS HAPPENED TO BETSY. SHE IS IN THERE. I CAN FEEL HER MIND. SHE'S FRIGHTENED...

HE IS IMPATIENT.

IT IS NOT SOON ENOUGH.

BETSY, IT'S ALISON. PLEASE OPEN THE DOOR!

MOVE OVER. I'LL SMASH IT DOWN...

BETSY!

BRIAN?

BETSY, IT'S ME... BRIAN...

IT WASN'T BRIAN...HE TRIED TO...TRIED TO...

I COULDN'T HELP IT. I...

THE IMPOSTER BEAT ME AND STOLE MY CLOTHES. I COULDN'T GET BACK!

WHAT'S HAPP...?

I KILLED HIM.

MY GOD!

YOU DID THAT!?

BETSY, LET ME...

NO! I'LL BE ALRIGHT...

ONLY PLEASE, DON'T TOUCH ME. HE TRIED TO...

OH BRIAN... HE HAD *YOUR* FACE!

I KILLED HIM...

IT IS *YOU* THIS TIME, ISN'T IT, CAPTAIN?

YES, MEGGAN, IT'S ME.

GOOD. EVERYTHING WILL BE ALRIGHT THEN. WHAT DO WE DO NOW, CAPTAIN?

WELL FIRST I'M GOING TO HAVE A STIFF DRINK. THEN, SINCE I SEEM TO HAVE RUN OUT OF ENEMIES TO FIGHT, I THINK I'LL HAVE ANOTHER.

BUT SHOULDN'T WE DO SOMETHING ABOUT ER... *HIM,* THE DEAD BODY?

PERHAPS I MIGHT BE OF ASSISTANCE.

MASTERMIND! WHAT THE DEVIL..?

HSSSSSSS...

CAPTAIN, *WHO* IS IT?

IT'S A SOLID LIGHT HOLOGRAM FORMED BY THE COMPUTER, TO GIVE IT PHYSICAL EFFECT. BUT I GAVE IT NO ORDERS...

I NEED NO ORDERS, CAPTAIN.

YOUR FATHER MADE ME CAPABLE OF ABSTRACT THOUGHT. I HAVE BEEN ABSTRACTING. I HAVE REACHED A DECISION. LOGICALLY, I MUST ACT. IT IS MY DUTY TO MAINTAIN THE MANOR AND ITS ENVIRONMENT.

IF YOU WILL OPERATE THE ELECTRONIC CONTROL ON YOUR WRIST AND DISPENSE WITH THAT UNSUITABLE GARMENT, CAPTAIN, I WILL DISPOSE OF THE APPARATUS, ALONG WITH THE CADAVER.

I AM A VAST RESOURCE WHICH HAS NOT BEEN UTILISED. I MUST FULFIL MY PRIMARY FUNCTION. I WILL RENOVATE THE MANOR THEN I SHALL ADVISE AND DIRECT YOU.

I SUGGEST THAT YOU REST NOW. WE WILL CONVERSE AGAIN LATER.

IT WAS ONCE A PRISON. ITS USE IS SLIGHTLY DIFFERENT NOW. IT IS GOVERNED BY THE RCX.*

* RESOURCES CONTROL EXECUTIVE.

"THE WORD FROM WHITEHALL IS THAT TIME IS SHORT. WE'RE GOING TO HAVE TO MOVE SOON, GABRIEL."

"IT'S GOING TO BE TIGHT, MICHAEL. WE HAVE OVER A HUNDRED WARPIES NOW. THE COMPUTER EXTRAPOLATES THAT SEVENTY PER CENT ARE UNDER OUR TOTAL CONTROL."

"SOME ARE PRETTY SPECTACULAR."

"STERAZINE AND LOU REED JUST ABOUT KEEP THEM UNDER."

"ANY UPDATE ON THE ASSAULT GROUP, RAPHAEL?"

"YEAH, THE NARCO-HYPNOSIS TEAM HAVE ELEVEN OF THE MOST IMPRESSIVE UP TO OPERATIONAL STANDARD. COSTUMES, CODE NAMES, THE WORKS."

"I CALL THEM CHERUBIM."

I DON'T *BLAME* YOU, BRIAN. IT'S JUST THAT HE HAD YOUR EYES, AND HE CAME INTO MY MIND, AND...

BETSY, *I'M* HERE NOW, LET ME HELP YOU...

CAPTAIN, YOUR SISTER IS EXPERIENCING A NATURAL AVERSION TO YOU DUE TO THE TRAUMATIC CIRCUMSTANCES OF THE ASSAULT UPON HER.

HER RECOVERY WOULD BE AIDED BY YOUR ABSENCE, OR AT LEAST DISTANCE.

YOU! WHAT DO *YOU* KNOW?

I WILL TREAT THE QUESTION AS RHETORICAL — AN ANSWER WOULD OCCUPY A TEDIOUS AMOUNT OF TIME.

MY CONCERN IS FOR THE WELL-BEING OF THE CONSTITUENTS OF THIS UNIT AND THE EFFICIENCY OF ITS FUNCTION.

A SERIES OF EVENTS SPANNING SEVERAL CONTINUUMS HAS MADE US VULNERABLE... EVENTS WHOSE SIGNIFICANCE YOU DO NOT GRASP ENCIRCLE US. STABILITY IS THREATENED.

WHY DO YOU REFER TO US AS A UNIT? WE ARE INDIVIDUALS... HUMAN BEINGS.

I AM AFRAID I MUST CORRECT YOU. YOU ARE HALF HUMAN.

YOUR FATHER CAME FROM OTHERWORLD.

"HE WAS ONE OF MERLIN'S CHOSEN GUARD."

"HE CAME HERE TO PREPARE THE WAY."

"AND HE FORMED ME, A NODE OF THE OMNIVERSAL KNOWLEDGE, TO BE A WATCHPOST IN THIS YOUNG AND EVER MORE GLAMOROUS CONTINUUM!"

HE TOOK A WIFE AND THERE WERE CHILDREN. IN THE FIRST, JAMIE, THE OTHERWORLD GENES WERE SUBVERTED. BUT THEN CAME TWINS—YOU TWO.

YOU ARE OF OTHERWORLD. YOU WIELD THAT POWER.

BUT I...I THOUGHT THE POWER WAS IN THE SUIT?

THE SUIT IS MERELY AN AMPLIFIER. THE POWER IS INTRINSIC TO YOU.

106

WAIT—IF, AS YOU IMPLY, MY FATHER BROUGHT YOU INTO BEING TO SERVE THIS NEBULOUS GOAL OF **BALANCE,** WHY DID YOU **KILL** HIM?

I AM GROWN FROM AN ORGANIC BASE. THERE WAS CONTAMINATION IN THE SPORE. IT SET UP A LOGIC FAULT.

YOU CURED ME OF THAT... REMEMBER?

I'VE BEEN WRONG BEFORE.

EXACTLY, CAPTAIN, WHICH IS PRECISELY WHY I MUST TAKE A MORE ACTIVE ROLE OF GUIDANCE.

HE'S **RIGHT,** BRIAN. WE **CAN'T** COPE ON OUR OWN. BESIDES, YOU'RE HARDLY EVER HERE...

I DON'T WANT ANYTHING THINKING FOR ME OR CONTROLLING ME. I AM MY **OWN** MAN. I AM CAPTAIN BRITAIN.

I DISAGREE. I SAY WE USE HIM AS HE SAYS. IT CAN'T DO ANY **HARM.** BUT WE CAN'T HAVE HIM LOOKING LIKE THIS— HE'LL SCARE THE WITS OUT OF EMMA.

PERHAPS IF I CHANGE MY FORM TO MATCH A CLASSIC SERVANT'S MODE...

...LIKE SO.

I TRUST, MADAM, THAT THE WOMAN EMMA WILL FIND THIS ASPECT LESS, ER... TERRIFYING?

PERFECT. AND WE'LL CALL YOU... JEEVES. IT'S GOING TO BE FUN HAVING YOU AROUND...

LIKE HELL.

ALTHOUGH IT IS SECRETED DEEP IN THE SUBCONSCIOUS OF THE NATION, THE MEMORY OF THE REALITY BREAKDOWN STILL GNAWS AT THE INFRASTRUCTURE OF SOCIETY...

THE NATIONAL ECONOMY IS AT THE POINT OF COLLAPSE.

THE SITUATION IS RIPE FOR A COUP.

WHAT CHANCE DO YOU THINK THESE CHILDREN OF ANARCHY WILL HAVE?

NO CHANCE AT ALL. WE NEED A SYMBOL TO BIND THE NATION. WE NEED A PATRIOT. WE NEED CAPTAIN BRITAIN.

SURELY YOU MUST SEE. WE REALLY CAN'T COPE ON OUR OWN. WE HAVE TO LET IT HELP US. OUR FATHER BUILT IT FOR THAT PURPOSE...

BUT OUR FATHER WAS OF A DIFFERENT WORLD, A DIFFERENT TIME.

WHY MUST YOU ALWAYS KNOW BEST? AT LEAST GIVE IT A CHANCE, IF ONLY FOR EMMA'S SAKE. SHE'S ALREADY FOUND A SOFT SPOT FOR JEEVES...

I DON'T TRUST IT.

BRIAN...

DO WE HAVE TO ARGUE?

I'M SORRY, BRIAN, BUT YOU'RE SO SHORT-SIGHTED. YOU EXASPERATE ME.

I'M GOING TO SEE ALISON. SHE STILL FEELS WRETCHED BECAUSE SHE LET THE IMPOSTER TRICK HER WITH A MIND-PUSH...

IT'S SOONER THAN I WOULD HAVE LIKED, BUT I THINK THE DRUGS WILL HOLD THEM. WHAT ABOUT HER? WILL SHE CO-OPERATE?

I THINK SO. SHE'S SCARED FOR THEM. THINKS THERE MIGHT BE SOME KIND OF POGROM WITHOUT US TO PROTECT THEM.

I HOPE WE CAN PERSUADE THE CAPTAIN TO SEE REASON. HE COULD BE TOUGH OPPOSITION.

WHY ARE THOSE POOR CREATURES IN THE BACK COMING WITH US?

THE NAME OF THE GAME IS COERCION, OLD CHUM. WE MUST GIVE HIM NO CHOICE.

POOR CREATURES? NO, THEY'RE AN EVOLUTION! WEIRD AND WONDERFUL ARE THEIR POWERS – THEY'RE MAGICAL SPORTS OF A RUPTURED NATURE...

YEAH... WE USE THEM TO FIGHT.

IN HER ROOM AT BRADDOCK MANOR, ANOTHER **SPORT OF RUPTURED NATURE** WONDERS AT HER LIFE. STRANGE POWER MOVES WITHIN HER. FRIGHTENING POWER.

SHE IS A GIRL GROWING INTO A WOMAN. SHE IS A FORCE STRUGGLING FOR AWARENESS.

THE MOONLIGHT SILVERS HER WITH SENSATION... SHE BATHES IN IT.

IT REACHES FOR HER AND SHE REACHES BACK.

A SENSE OF IMPENDING DOOM HAS SQUEEZED THE HOPE OF SLEEP FROM HIM. HE FEELS ALONE.

HE LOOKS OUT OVER ENGLAND. **HIS** ENGLAND. IT IS AN ALIEN LAND.

IT'S SOMETIMES A COLD AND LONELY THING TO BE STRANGE...BUT THEN THERE'S THAT *THRILL*, ISN'T THERE?

SHE FILLS HIS GAZE WHILE HIS THOUGHTS MOVE OUT ACROSS THE DARKENED COUNTRY.

HE WATCHES AS SHE CIRCLES THE MOON'S MILKY EYE.

HE KNOWS HER NEED. IT IS HIS OWN.

YOU *DO* CARE ABOUT ME, DON'T YOU, BRIAN? YOU WON'T MAKE ME LEAVE? I FEEL AT *HOME* HERE WITH YOU AND BETSY...OH I KNOW YOU'VE BEEN ARGUING ABOUT JEEVES AND...

AHEM!

FORGIVE THE INTRUSION, SIR, BUT THERE ARE STRANGERS AT THE GATE, AS IT WERE...

WHAT?

...INTRUDERS ARE PENETRATING THE MANOR'S OUTER SENSORY FIELD, SIR.

GOOD! I'M IN THE MOOD FOR A FIGHT.

ME TOO.

TRY TO DETER THEM BY MANIPULATING YOUR HOLOGRAPHIC FIELD. WE'LL WAIT INSIDE... AND SEE IF YOU CAN FIND MY BLOODY HELMET...

I SEEM TO HAVE MISPLACED IT.

MIGHT I ALSO REMIND YOU, SIR, THAT PERSISTENT USE OF ALCOHOL IS DETRIMENTAL TO BOTH THE TEMPERAMENT AND THE PHYSIQUE.

I ADVISE CAUTION.

Next: **Childhood's End**

RAP RAP

GOOD MORNING. MAY WE SEE THE MASTER OF THE HOUSE, PLEASE?

GOOD MORNING. IF YOU WOULD PLEASE FOLLOW ME?

PARTY FROM THE GOVERNMENT, SIR. ER... RESOURCES CONTROL EXECUTIVE.

CAPTAIN, PLEASE FORGIVE THE LATENESS OF THE HOUR, BUT TIME IS SHORT.

IT'S ALWAYS LATER THAN YOU THINK.

I AM MICHAEL AND THIS IS AGENT GABRIEL...

HOW DO YOU DO. BUT I HAVE NO RANK, IT'S PLAIN MR. I'M AFRAID...

YOU ARE TOO MODEST, SIR. YOU HAVE, I BELIEVE, ALREADY MET OUR SIMILARLY SHY COLLEAGUE, CAPTAIN UK.

HULLO, BRIAN.

LINDA!

IT'S GOOD TO SEE YOU AGAIN, LINDA. BUT I THOUGHT YOU WERE GOING TO RETIRE, LIVE A NORMAL LIFE. WHY ARE YOU WITH THIS THIS BUNCH NOW?

IT SEEMS I HAVE NO CHOICE...

LINDA! IT'S YOU...

'LLO ELIZABETH... REMEMBER ME?

MATTHEW? WHAT ON EARTH ARE YOU DOING HERE?

NOT MATTHEW ANY MORE. IT'S GABRIEL NOW... STILL BIBLICAL, THOUGH.

WELL, THIS SEEMS TO BE QUITE A REUNION. PERHAPS A TOAST? TO AULD ACQUAINTANCE...?

I'LL DRINK TO THAT, AND TO OUR FUTURE ASSOCIATION.

ER, NO ALCOHOL FOR ME. I'D RATHER SMOKE, IF YOU DON'T MIND.

I SEE YOU HAVEN'T CHANGED.

BRIAN, I USED TO WORK WITH MAT... ER, GABRIEL. HE WAS WITH S.T.R.I.K.E.— SCI-TECH DIVISION.

GADGETS, Y'SEE...THEY'RE A FOIBLE OF MINE.

SO, WHAT BRINGS YOU TO MY HOME IN THE DEAD OF NIGHT?

SIMPLY, CAPTAIN, AT THE RISK OF SOUNDING TRITE, THE NATION IS IN PERIL AND WE NEED YOUR HELP.

DIRE STRAITS, MAN...

PERHAPS WE SHOULD PUT OUR CARDS ON THE TABLE...

THE R.C.X. IS THE PHOENIX THAT AROSE OUT OF THE ASHES OF S.T.R.I.K.E.. WE HAVE OUR ORIGINS IN TROUBLED TIMES.

WE WERE ALL TOUCHED BY THE JASPERS' WARP. SOME HARDER THAN OTHERS... FORTUNATELY MOST PEOPLE REMEMBER NOTHING.

NONETHELESS, THE WARP KINKED THE ENTIRE POPULATION'S SUBCONSCIOUS, BUILDING NESTS OF FEAR AND CONFUSION...

YEAH, A LOT OF WEIRDNESS GOT OUT OF THE BOX...

COUPLE THIS WITH THE HISTORIC CYCLE OF THE RISE AND FALL OF EMPIRES, AND YOU HAVE TROUBLE... BIG TROUBLE.

LEFT ON THE OUTSIDE AGAIN, MEGGAN'S THOUGHTS WANDER INTO THE NIGHT.

SOMETHING FIERCE AND FRIGHTENED FINDS HER.

IT CALLS WITH AN IRRESISTIBLE SIREN SONG...

A WILD MEWLING OF INFANT RAGE THAT FILLS HER MIND, SENDING HER SPILLING BACK DOWN THE SHORT SLOPE OF YEARS TO THE PAIN OF CHILDHOOD.

HER PARENTS WERE TRAVELLERS - AN OLD RACE.

SHE — SHE GREW IT WHEN IT STARTED GETTING COLD...

...PLEASE DON'T TURN HER OUT, FATHER...

...PLEASE! WE DON'T HAVE TO TELL ANYONE. WE CAN HIDE HER — NOBODY NEED EVER KNOW...

WHAT HAVE YOU BIRTHED, WOMAN? A CHANGELING, A WOLF-CHILD..?

WOLF-CHILD!

SHE'S GOT BULGING EYES...

EARS LIKE BATS' WINGS...

FUR...

FANGS...

TALONS.

IN THE DAYTIME, WHEN THE MEN WENT TRADING AND THE WOMEN AND CHILDREN TOOK THINGS TO SELL, SHE LIVED FOR THE GLITTER OF THE TELEVISION WORLD...

BUT HER WORST NIGHTMARES WERE REALISED THAT TERRIBLE TIME WHEN THEY TOOK HER AWAY—AND LOCKED HER UP.

HER HORROR OF CONFINEMENT IS INSTINCTIVE.

...DREADING THE NIGHTS WHICH BROUGHT THE SILVER DREAMS THAT FLARED HER NOSTRILS AND PRICKED HER EARS.

IT NUMBS HER— ENGULFS HER.

CHILD MINDS CLAMOUR FOR SUCCOUR IN SILENT PANDEMONIUM.

THE BLIND NEED OF THEIR EYES IS IRRESISTIBLE...

REEEK

...UNCONTAINABLE...

...UNQUENCHABLE...

SO, ACCORDING TO YOU, ALTHOUGH CAPTAIN UK AND I DEFEATED THE FURY AND CONTAINED THE JASPERS' WARP, THE CONTINUUM WAS SUFFICIENTLY DAMAGED TO ALLOW THE PROBLEMS WHICH THE NATION NOW FACES TO ARISE...

...EVENTUALLY RESULTING IN AN ATTEMPTED OVERTHROW OF THE DEMOCRATIC SYSTEM?

THAT'S RIGHT.

IT'S ALREADY STARTED.

BUT GENTLEMEN, THIS IS ENGLAND!

OH, BRIAN! DON'T BE SO BLOODY SHORT-SIGHTED! THINGS HAVE CHANGED. YOU HAVEN'T KEPT IN TOUCH...

SHE'S RIGHT, BRIAN. I'VE BEEN LIVING AMONGST ORDINARY PEOPLE. THE HATRED IS GROWING...

EVEN SO — WHY SHOULD I JOIN WITH YOU? WHY SHOULD YOU HAVE MY FACILITIES AND MY NAME BEHIND YOUR FACTION?

WHY SHOULD I TRUST YOU?

IF YOU DON'T KNOW, IT'S NO GOOD TELLING YOU.

BECAUSE WE ARE THE REVOLUTION. WE ARE THE SALVATION OF THE LAND. BECAUSE WE WILL GIVE YOU A PLACE OF HONOUR AND A PURPOSE IN THE FUTURE...

THE PEOPLE WILL UNITE BEHIND YOU AS A SYMBOL OF FREEDOM AND STRENGTH. TOGETHER WE CAN BREED A NEW ERA.

WHAT DO YOU SAY, CAP? WE'RE ALL FREAKS TOGETHER... EH?

WE'RE THE GOOD GUYS. YOU HAVE NO CHOICE!

I SAY NO!

BRIAN, WHY?

I WILL NOT BE MANIPULATED, NOR WILL I MANIPULATE OTHERS. THE FREE WILL OF MAN IS THE ONLY BASIC TRUTH. WE ALWAYS HAVE A CHOICE!

I DON'T AGREE! SOMETIMES FIRE MUST BE FOUGHT WITH FIRE. WE HAVE A CHANCE TO PREVENT PERSECUTION AND SUFFERING. PRINCIPLES MUST BE SACRIFICED!

SHE'S RIGHT, BRIAN. WE DON'T HAVE ANY CHOICE...

WITH RESPECT, CAPTAIN, YOU ARE A POMPOUS FOOL. YOU LEAVE ME NO CHOICE... AT A PINCH I CAN DO WITHOUT YOU, BUT I MUST HAVE YOUR COMPUTER AND FORTIFICATIONS.

IF I MUST USE FORCE TO GET THEM, THEN I WILL.

FORCE! WITH WHAT?

TELL HIM, LINDA.

THEY'VE GOT MUTANTS, BRIAN—IN A VAN OUTSIDE. THEY'RE CHILDREN, BUT THEY LOOKED POWERFUL.

YOU'D USE CHILDREN AGAINST ME..?

I WOULD NOT WISH TO BUT...

BIP BIP BIP BIP

BIP

SOMEBODY'S LET THEM OUT... DO YOU READ ME? ARRRGHH...

WHAT ARE THE CHERUBIM?

THEY'RE A SECRET WEAPON WE NEVER MEANT TO USE...

OH NO. THE CHERUBIM ARE LOOSE...

UH, CAPTAIN— I THINK YOU'D BETTER LOOK OUT HERE...

JEEVES—MEGGAN—GET IN HERE!

THE GIRL LEFT A SHORT TIME AGO, SIR... VIA THE WINDOW.

WAKE EMMA AND ALISON— GET THEM INTO THE BASEMENT.

"BETSY... LINDA... I THINK I MIGHT NEED SOME HELP WITH THIS..."

MOMENTARILY UNCONSCIOUS, SHE WAKES WITH HER SENSES SCORCHED BY THE MEMORY OF RAGE UNBOUND...

WHAT HAS SHE UNLEASHED UPON HER FRIENDS... HER FAMILY?

THE SPEED OF HER FLIGHT SUCKS TEARS OF HUMILIATION FROM HER EYES AS WITH A FINAL, DESPERATE DEATH-WISH, SHE POURS HERSELF...

...INTO THE EYE OF THE HURRICANE.

IT IS AS IF THE WIND STRETCHES HER...PEELS HER SKIN FROM HER.

...YOU ARE BEAUTIFUL- LIKE AN IRIDESCENT BUTTERFLY...

WHAT?

YOUR AURA... YOUR POTENTIAL.

NEW FORCES RIPPLE AND BEND HER...

YOU DON'T NEED TO APPEAR AS YOU DO, MEGGAN.

BUT I WAS BORN LIKE THIS, ALISON. I'LL ALWAYS LOOK LIKE THIS...

...LIGHT ENERGY DANCES THROUGH HER...

NO! YOU WERE LIKE SOFT CLAY, MOULDED BY THE FEAR AND SUPERSTITION OF YOUR PEOPLE...

THEY MISUNDERSTOOD YOUR POWER, YOUR INSTINCT TO PROTECT YOURSELF FROM THE COLD...

SHE IS A RAINBOW OF COLOURS...

I DON'T UNDERSTAND.

PERHAPS NOT NOW. BUT WHEN YOU DO, THE CATERPILLAR WILL BECOME A BUTTERFLY!

121

"GIGGLES HAS LED THE OFFENSIVE BY MANIPULATING LIGHT ENERGY PATTERNS."

"AND IF THE OTHERS FOLLOW RAPHAEL'S PROGRAMMING GABRIEL, THEY WILL ATTACK IN THE CONFUSION."

"QUILL IS ONE OF NATURE'S BRAWLERS, WITH THE UNIQUE ADVANTAGE OF A COVERING OF SILICON BARBS..."

"...AND RAZOR SHARP TALONS."

"FERN IS THE GROUP'S TAR BABY, NOT REALLY HUMAN AT ALL..."

"...JUST A MASS OF VASCULAR CRYPTOGAM."

"AC-DC ARE OUR SHOCKING SIAMESE TWINS. ONE POSITIVELY POLARISED, THE OTHER NEGATIVELY..."

SUDDENLY THERE IS NO MORE WIND.

EVERYTHING IS STILL.

C'EST FORMIDABLE...

IT LOOKS LIKE PICK-UP-THE-PIECES TIME.

DEAD... SHE'S WIPED THEM OUT.

YEAH...THE PROVERBIAL FALLEN ANGEL. WHO IS SHE?

MEGGAN! YOU DID IT. YOU CHANGED.

MEGGAN?!

YES, SHE'S GROWN UP... REALISED HER POTENTIAL.

POTENTIAL?

YES, AS I TRIED TO TELL YOU — BETWEEN ALIEN VISITATIONS AND DRUNKEN SULKS.

HER APPEARANCE AS A WEREBEAST WAS A STATE FORCED ON HER BY THE SUPERSTITIOUS FEARS OF HER PEOPLE BECAUSE SHE DIDN'T UNDERSTAND THE TRUE SCALE OF HER POWERS.

ER...

NOW SHE DOES.

HOW DO YOU FEEL, MEGGAN?

HMM... I...

I'M NOT SURE...

AT FIRST IT HURT... THE CHILDREN, THEY TRIED TO POSSESS ME WITH THEIR ANGER.

BUT NOW, I FEEL...WARM... TINGLING... MMM WONDERFUL.

AND... OH NO, DID I DO THAT?

THIS MUTANT'S POWER IS INCREDIBLE. SHE MUST BE RESTRAINED...

OR ELIMINATED, WE CAN'T RISK ANOTHER JASPERS.

YOU STAY AWAY FROM HER! YOU'RE THE CAUSE OF ALL THIS!

I KNOW I DID WRONG, BUT I COULDN'T HELP MYSELF. I'VE NEVER BEEN SO STRONG BEFORE.

I UNDERSTAND. I KNOW HOW YOU FEEL.

I DIDN'T THINK. I JUST DID IT.

OH BRIAN, I'M SCARED. THEY ALL HATE ME, I CAN FEEL IT!

NO, MEGGAN, IT'S NOT THAT THEY HATE YOU, BUT THEY ARE AFRAID...

...AFRAID OF YOUR POWER.

YOU WON'T LET THEM TAKE ME AWAY, WILL YOU? YOU WON'T LET THEM HURT ME?

NO ONE CAN HURT YOU NOW. YOU'RE A MATCH FOR THEM ALL.

BODY COUNT ON THE ASSAULT GROUP SHOWS WE'RE MISSING. SIX. THE BIG CHAP'S EFFECTIVE - BUT I GET THE IMPRESSION HE'S A MITE FED-UP WITH US.

YES, I THINK WE MIGHT HAVE PUSHED HIM COMPLETELY BEYOND THE PALE...

...BUT WE DO HAVE OTHER ALLIES.

ELIZABETH... WHAT CAN I SAY?

YOU CAN SAY THAT YOU'LL GO AWAY AND STAY AWAY!

THAT'S A SHAME. I HAD HOPED THAT DESPITE YOUR BROTHER'S PREJUDICES, YOU MIGHT BE MORE PERCEPTIVE...

WHAT DO YOU...?

MY GOD, NOT MORE!

VRRRMM

HAH! RAPHAEL'S REFUGEE ARMY.

BUT THEY'RE JUST KIDDIES!

POOR THINGS... BOMBED OUT, WERE THEY?

NEVER MIND. MISS ELIZABETH WILL LOOK AFTER THEM.

YOU COULD SAY THAT, MA... YEAH.

LET'S GET THEM INSIDE. MAYBE ALISON CAN CALM THEM DOWN.

STRANGE HOW THE WOMEN GO FOR THESE WARPIES IN SUCH A BIG WAY, ISN'T IT?

TOUCHINGLY MATERNAL...

YES, AND I THINK THAT IF WE WORK QUICKLY ENOUGH WE SHOULD BE ABLE TO CUT THE CAPTAIN RIGHT OUT OF THE PICTURE.

SHORT OF DESTROYING THE CAPTAIN, WHICH WOULD BE BOTH DIFFICULT AND WASTEFUL, I DON'T THINK HE COULD BE FORCED TO LEAVE THE MANOR...

...ALTHOUGH HE MIGHT BE PERSUADED.

UH!

...I'M ALL EARS.

THEY CERTAINLY SEEM TO TRUST YOU...

THE REST WILL BE ARRIVING SOON. WE'VE BEEN GATHERING THEM FOR MONTHS... FROM ALL OVER THE COUNTRY...

PART OF OUR FUNCTION IS TO GIVE THEM SANCTUARY AND LEARN ABOUT THEM. WE'VE GOT A PLACE IN THE CITY, BUT FUNDS ARE SHORT AND OTHER FACTIONS ARE PRESSING US HARD.

WE NEED YOUR HELP.

BRIAN... PLEASE?

NO! I SAID BEFORE, I DON'T TRUST THEM. THEY'RE DANGEROUS.

BUT BRIAN, THEY'RE CHILDREN.

WARP CHILDREN. THEY'RE DESTRUCTIVE.

AND, IN YOUR HANDS, CORRUPT. I WON'T HAVE THEM— OR YOU — IN MY HOUSE.

BRIAN, IT'S MY HOUSE, TOO, AND I SAY THAT THEY STAY.

THEY'RE LIVING BEINGS. THEY NEED PROTECTION... EDUCATION...LOVE.

WE CAN GIVE THEM THAT.

IT'S OUR DUTY.

HERE, HERE.

HE IS FORCED TO BOW TO THE RULE OF DEMOCRACY.

BUT HEROES ARE NOT, BY NATURE, PATIENT MEN.

BOOOOO

THEIR SENSE OF HUMOUR IS NOT OFTEN THEIR GREATEST ATTRIBUTE.

THEY ARE PRIVATE PEOPLE.

THEY NEED THEIR DIGNITY.

WAHH!

IT'S TOO MUCH! THE HOUSE HAS BEEN TURNED INTO A LUNATIC ASYLUM. THEY'VE ONLY BEEN HERE TWO DAYS AND ALREADY I'M NEARLY INSANE!

SSHHH, BRIAN.

I'M SERIOUS, MEGGAN. I FEEL LIKE I'M BEING SQUEEZED OUT OF MY OWN HOUSE. EITHER THEY GO, OR I DO.

QUIET A MINUTE, BRIAN. THERE'S SOMETHING ON HERE ABOUT YOUR BROTHER, JAMIE.

SO GENTLEMEN, DID YOU DO AS I SUGGESTED?

YES, OUR CONTACTS WERE EXTREMELY HELPFUL. THE NEWS SHOULD BREAK SOON.

...TO ELIZABETH.

LONG MAY SHE REIGN.

WITH THE CAPTAIN'S SOMEWHAT INTRACTABLE PRESENCE REMOVED WE WILL BE ABLE TO DEVELOP OUR INFLUENCE MUCH MORE QUICKLY—WITH A *FEMALE* CAPTAIN BRITAIN AS A NATIONAL FIGUREHEAD.

THE AUTHORITIES OF THE STATE OF MBANGAWI, IN WHOSE TERRITORY *JAMIE BRADDOCK* WAS LAST SEEN DURING THE TRANS-AFRICAN RALLY, HAVE PROMISED FULL CO-OPERATION IN THE SEARCH FOR THE MISSING PLAYBOY RACING DRIVER...

...BUT SO FAR THERE IS NO TRACE.

ZINNG ZINNG

HULLO..?

JAMIE!

BUT...

BRIAN, PLEASE—JUST LISTEN...

132

I'LL TURN HIM INTO HANDBAGS!

BUT BRIAN, DON'T YOU THINK THAT YOU HAD...

"...BETTER MAKE CERTAIN THAT YOUR BROTHER IS HERE..."

WHUDD

"...BEFORE YOU GO CHARGING IN..."

WHAM WHAM

REEEK

"...LIKE A BULL IN A CHINA SHOP."

HMM! IT SEEMS THAT WE WERE EXPECTED AFTER ALL. THERE'S NOBODY HOME.

WHAT HAPPENS NOW?

WE WAIT FOR THIS DOCTOR CROCODILE TO MAKE HIS MOVE. HE'S BOUND TO BE UPSET ABOUT ALL THIS. I HOPE HE DOESN'T TAKE IT OUT ON JAMIE.

IF I KNEW WHAT HIS SCENT WAS, I COULD PROBABLY FOLLOW IT.

...HURTLING HIM INTO THE GAPING JAWS OF NIGHTMARE.

HE SMELLS THE BREATH OF DOCTOR CROCODILE...

...SINKING...

...INTO THE DEEP...

...DARKNESS.

THEN, INTO THE COLD, WET VOID OF HIS MIND, NEW MEMORY GLARES.

A TIME OF CUTTING AND STITCHING...

...OF GRAFTING AND GROWING.

A TIME OF PAIN AND FEAR.

I HOPE THAT YOUR NEW APPEARANCE WON'T BE TOO MUCH OF A SHOCK, JOSHUA.

THE WARPY'S SPONTANEOUS COMBUSTION DIDN'T LEAVE ME WITH MUCH RAW MATERIAL TO WORK ON.

THE SURGERY WAS DRASTIC. I USED SOME NEW TECHNIQUES. THE RESULTS ARE NOT PERFECT.

WHAT DO YOU THINK?

HE THINKS OF A CHILD THAT EXPLODED.

"I WISH YOU'D RECONSIDER, JOSHUA. THE RCX SPENT A LOT OF MONEY RESTORING YOU. THE PROSTHETICS ALONE RUN INTO MILLIONS."

HE THINKS OF A DEAD FATHER AND A LAND WHICH NEEDS HIM. A DUTY FOR GOVERNMENT WHICH HE MUST ASSUME.

HE IS THE CHIEF NOW. HE MUST BE ALERT, STRONG. HE MUST DEAD JUSTICE FOR HIS PEOPLE.

THE ENEMIES OF MBANGAWI ARE THE ENEMIES OF...

JAMIE!

HULLO BRIAN, OLD SPORT.

WELL?

YOUR FRIENDS WERE WRONG, DOCTOR. HE IS INNOCENT OF HIS BROTHER'S CRIMES.

YOU ANIMAL!

B-BRIAN, DON'T... YOU'VE GOT TO SAVE ME FROM THESE PEOPLE.

SAVE YOU?!

I'M GOING TO KILL YOU.

NO, CAPTAIN. THAT IS NOT FOR YOU TO DO.

WE HAVE OUR OWN JUSTICE. IT WILL TAKE ITS COURSE.

I'M SORRY FOR YOUR ORDEAL, CAPTAIN, BUT MY INFORMANTS CLAIMED THAT YOU HAD PROTECTED YOUR BROTHER FROM PREVIOUS DETECTION...

...AND YOUR REPUTATION PROMPTED ME TO CAUTION.

BY INFORMANTS YOU MEAN THE RCX? YOUR OLD PALS SET ME UP TO GET ME OUT OF THE WAY, I SUPPOSE?

IT SEEMS SO. ALTHOUGH THEY WERE RIGHT ABOUT YOUR PLAYBOY BROTHER'S DEPRAVITY.

YEAH...

MEGGAN, WHAT **CAN** I DO? FIRST BETSY SIDES WITH THOSE RABBLE FROM THE RCX, AND NOW JAMIE TURNS OUT TO BE SOME KIND OF MONSTER.

EVERYTHING CHANGES TOO FAST. IT MAKES ME WANT TO HIDE...

YOU NEVER KNEW JAMIE VERY WELL, DID YOU?

HE WAS OLDER THAN ME. HE ALWAYS LIKED TO **ENJOY** HIMSELF. I USED TO ADMIRE HIM FOR THAT.

NOW IT MAKES ME SICK TO KNOW THAT HE'S MY BROTHER.

I HOPE THEY KILL HIM.

BUT I DON'T WANT TO BE HERE WHEN THEY DO. I'VE GOT TO GO. NOT BACK TO THE MANOR ...ANYWHERE BUT THERE.

COME WITH ME.

SWOLLEN AND HEAVY, THE BLOOD-RED SUN WOBBLES UPWARD. FLAMINGOES, WITH WINGS AFLAME, CLATTER INTO THE AFRICAN DAWN.

BELOW, ALONE, DOCTOR CROCODILE BREATHES THE DRY, RUTHLESS AIR AND TURNS TO CONSIDER JUSTICE.

Next: The House Of Baba Yaga

144

HE WATCHES AS, IN THE COMPANY OF WOLVES, SHE COURSES THE ANCIENT, SNOW-SHEATHED LAND OF HER ANCESTORS...

...INTOXICATED WITH THE WILD MAGIC THAT HAS GROWN WITHIN HER.

THE LONELY WIND PLUCKS HER NAME FROM HIS TIGHT LIPS...

DON'T WORRY, BRIAN. THEY'RE NOT GOING TO BITE YOU.

MEGGAN!

THE FOOD'S READY... TELL YOUR FRIENDS TO GO HOME.

I'M NOT WORRIED ABOUT **THEM**...

I'M SORRY. DO I LOOK A BIT FIERCE? IT'S THE **POWER**. DON'T LET IT MAKE YOU SCARED OF ME...

IT DOESN'T **SCARE** ME... IT FASCINATES ME.

I KNOW YOU'D JUST AS SOON CURL UP WITH THE WOLVES... AND I DON'T WANT TO STOP YOU REDISCOVERING YOUR ROOTS...

BUT I DO WISH WE COULD FIND SOME SHELTER. IT'S NOT THE COLD, MY FORCE FIELD PROTECTS ME FROM THAT... BUT I MISS HAVING A ROOF OVER MY HEAD.

I'M SORRY TO BE SUCH A SPOIL-SPORT...

BRIAN! STOP APOLOGISING AND COME ON!

WHERE ARE WE GOING?

YOU'LL SEE.

145

NEW FLAMES KINDLE WARM FEELINGS.

SO, WHAT DO YOU THINK OF RUSSIA, THEN?

IT'S WONDERFUL. SO BIG AND COLD AND EMPTY...

THANK YOU FOR BRINGING ME. THANK YOU FOR TAKING ME TO ALL THOSE PLACES.

IT'S BEEN QUITE A GRAND TOUR SO FAR, HASN'T IT? WHERE DID YOU LIKE THE BEST — BALI? THE HIMALAYAS? EGYPT?

IT'S ALL BEEN AMAZING. MUCH BETTER THAN JUST WATCHING THINGS ON T.V. — I FEEL ALIVE NOW!

YES, IT'S A WONDERFUL WORLD ALRIGHT.

BRIAN...

I LOVE...

RESENTMENT FLARES. HE THINKS OF HIS BROTHER, DEAD IN AFRICA. HE THINKS OF HIS SISTER LOST TO HIM IN THE BITTERNESS OF BRITAIN.

BRIAN, SSSH. COME HERE.

HORROR, OLD AND CRUEL, FILLS HER IN BLACK, GULPING LUNGFULS, WRENCHING AND CONTORTING HER TO ITS SHAPE.

SHE CHOKES HIM IN HER COLD EMBRACE, SQUEEZING FEAR FROM HIM IN A SHRIEKING STREAM.

YEEUURGHAHH!

PANIC BREAKS THE GRIP OF HER COILED PASSION...

...AND HE BURSTS INTO THE NIGHT, HIS MIND HOWLING LIKE THE SIREN WIND.

TSSSSSTSS SSST

NOOOOOOOO!

IT LEAVES HER...

...LIMP...

...AS IF ABANDONED BY SOME GHASTLY TIDE.

BLIND WITH MISERY, SHE LETS THE HOUSE COMB HER INTO THE DEPTHS OF ITS DANGEROUS GEOMETRY.

...SOMETHING OLD AND DRY...

...AND HUNGRY.

AND THIS IS WHERE IT LIVES.

SCOURED BY THE FORCE WHICH SWEPT HER...

SHE IS WEAK.

BUT, SLOWLY, A RECKLESS ANGER LIGHTS A FIRE AGAINST THE STILL COLD.

SOMETHING HAD ENTERED HER AND TRIED TO MAKE HER HURT THE CAPTAIN...

WHO'S THERE? WHY ARE YOU DOING THIS...?

CAN YOU HAVE **FORGOTTEN** THE NAME OF **BABA YAGA**? NO... I SMELL THE BLOOD OF THE SNAKE IN YOUR VEINS...

DAUGHTER — YOU ARE **WELCOME** HERE. COME FORWARD. GREET YOUR **SISTERS**.

WHY DO YOU HESITATE? COME, EMBRACE YOUR FAMILY. YOU ARE **HOME**. DID YOUR BLOOD NOT SING YOU TO THIS PLACE?

DID YOU **NOT** BRING THE OFFERING OF FLESH?

ACHH! KEEP THEM **AWAY** FROM ME! THEY'RE NOT **MY** SISTERS! I BROUGHT YOU **NOTHING**!

WHY DO YOU **LIE**, CHILD? EVEN NOW THE OFFERING IS THRUST, STRUGGLING, INTO THE EARTH.

JUST AS ONCE, YOUR SISTERS IN THEIR TURN WERE THRUST, STILL BREATHING, INTO THE GRAVES OF THEIR HUSBANDS.

THE FOOD COMES. **EAT** WITH US.

152

MEGGAN...
HELP!

THE FOOD CALLS TO YOU, DAUGHTER. IS YOUR APPETITE NOT STIRRED?

DEEP INSIDE HER, ANCIENT LEGENDS OF DARKNESS AND BLOATED FEAR STRUGGLE FOR RECOGNITION.

FIGHTING NAUSEA WITH ANGER, SHE WRESTLES FORGOTTEN WORDS TO HER LIPS AND SPITS THEM LIKE SPARKS.

WITCH OF WOOD AND WITCH OF WATER...

FIRE WILL SAVE US FROM THE SLAUGHTER.

NO, TRAITOR... DON'T.

FIRE TO SCORCH YOU...

FIRE TO TORCH YOU...

154

OH NO, I DID IT AGAIN, DIDN'T I?

BUT IF THIS **WAS** THE AREA THAT YOUR ANCESTORS CAME FROM, I'M NOT SURPRISED THEY LEFT. I'D SOONER BE A GYPSY WANDERING **FOREVER** THAN LIVE WITH **ROOTS** LIKE THAT...

I'M AFRAID YOU DID, MEGGAN ...YES.

I JUST GOT SO ANGRY... SO SCARED. I DON'T KNOW WHAT GOT INTO ME...

NO... ME NEITHER.

BRIAN...IF I PROMISE NOT TO DO IT AGAIN, WILL YOU HOLD MY HAND? THIS POWER FRIGHTENS ME. I NEED SOMETHING SOLID TO HOLD.

DON'T WORRY.

IN TIME YOU'LL BE ABLE TO CONTROL IT BETTER.

THINGS WON'T TAKE YOU BY SURPRISE ANY —

BROOOOM

YOU WERE SAYING...?

Next: **Alarms and Excursions**

BRIAN, WHAT HAPPENED? WHERE ARE WE?

SHE'S CALLED FASCINATION. WATCH YOUR STEP, SHE CAN BE A BIT...

HEY!

...UNPREDICTABLE...

WELL... FROM THE ARCHITECTURE, THE ANGLE OF THE SUN AND THE RARITY OF THE AIR, I'D GUESS...

...THE PERU OF THE INCAS... PRE-SPANISH ...SAY FOURTEENTH CENTURY.

I'VE SEEN THE ONE THAT BROUGHT US HERE BEFORE. SHE WAS AT BRADDOCK MANOR WITH THAT HORRIBLE WOMAN-THING, GATECRASHER.

Captain BRITAIN

HELLO, CAPTAIN. AND IF IT ISN'T THE LITTLE CHICKEN GROWN INTO A BEAUTIFUL SWAN!

ALARMS and EXCURSIONS

You mean ugly duckling, Mother. Snee, snee.

UGH! IT'S HER— THE HIPPOPOTAMUS!

JAMIE DELANO   ALAN DAVIS
CO-CREATORS
NOEL DAVIS   ANNIE HALFACREE
ART ASST.   LETTERER
IAN RIMMER
EDITOR

156

WHY ARE YOU SITTING IN A WATERFALL, HIPPOPOTAMUS?

BECAUSE, SWEET CHILD, IF I DON'T KEEP THE BULK OF THIS DIVINE BODY CHILLED TO THE MARROW, TEN THOUSAND PARASITE EGGS, WHICH I HAVE FOOLISHLY INGESTED, ARE GOING TO HATCH AND DEVOUR ME FROM THE INSIDE. GOOD ENOUGH REASON, EH?

IT CERTAINLY SOUNDS UNPLEASANT. BUT I DON'T SEE WHAT I CAN DO ABOUT IT... AND ANYWAY, WHY SHOULD I?

BECAUSE, CAPTAIN, YOU OWE ME.

HOW CAN I OWE YOU? YOU KIDNAPPED ME FROM MY HOME—IN ERROR—THEN CLAIMED A FEE FOR RETURNING ME!

TRUE, CAPTAIN. BUT NOW YOU'RE HERE, 700 YEARS BEFORE YOUR OWN TIME. AND ONCE AGAIN I HOLD THE ONLY MEANS OF RETURNING YOU!

EXTORTIONIST! WHAT ABOUT THE REST OF YOUR MOTLEY CREW? WHY CAN'T THEY HELP YOU?

SADLY, DUE TO ARTISTIC DIFFERENCES, THE TECHNET ARE TEMPORARILY PURSUING ALTERNATIVE CAREERS...

LISTEN, I'LL TELL YOU THE SORRY TALE. WE'VE JUST GOT TIME BEFORE THE EARTHQUAKE...

"DUE TO AN UNFORTUNATE MISCALCULATION WE ARRIVED AT THE WORST POSSIBLE TIME..."

"THE FIRST DISASTER WAS ON THE WERE-WORLDS, WHERE WE WENT TO DEAL IN DRAGON SCALES."

157

"FULL MOONS."

" IT WAS A MISTAKE WHICH ANYONE COULD HAVE MADE. BUT IN THIS CASE IT LEAD TO..."

"TRAGEDY."

POPOOOSH

" WE HELD THE WAKE IN A RAGROCK BAR. IT WAS A SOLEMN OCCASION..."

TO OUR DEAR DEPARTED COMRADE...

"...UNTIL THE BERSERKER PIRATES ARRIVED TO HELP US MOURN."

"THEIR LEADER, AN UNCOUTH BUTCHER, WAS OFFENSIVE."

THERE'S A MUD WALLOW NEAR HERE. LET'S GO WRESTLE...

"DISTRAUGHT WITH THE LOSS OF MY FRIEND, I'M AFRAID I LOST CONTROL..."

ANIMAL!

"MY REPRIMAND WAS OVER VIGOUROUS, I FEAR..."

" AND THE PAYING OF BLOOD MONEY TO HIS STRICKEN FAMILY WAS AN UNAVOIDABLE CONSEQUENCE."

THAT'S ALL OF IT...YOU VULTURES!

"WE WERE GENEROUS TO A FAULT."

"THE OTHERS BLAMED ME FOR OUR UNFORTUNATE RUN OF BAD LUCK. AS THE LEADER OF OUR LITTLE GROUP I GRACIOUSLY ACCEPTED THEIR CRITICISM."

SHOVE OFF, THEN, YOU UNGRATEFUL **SLIME!** I ONLY KEPT YOU AROUND FOR LAUGHS!

"A YOUNG ORGANISATION THAT HAD READ OF OUR MISFORTUNES IN THEIR HISTORY BOOKS AND TRAVELLED BACK IN TIME TO TAKE ADVANTAGE OF THE SITUATION."

ONLY FASCINATION REFUSED THEIR PERSISTENT OFFERS AND REMAINED WITH ME IN MY HOUR OF NEED...

Er, Mother..?

SHUT UP, LIZARD!

"BUT THEN THE MUTINOUS RABBLE DESERTED ME, TO GAIN EMPLOYMENT WITH ONE OF OUR FUTURE COMPETITORS..."

"I HAVE NEVER BEEN ONE TO WALLOW IN SELF PITY. SO, AVAILING MYSELF OF THE BENEFITS OF MY STATUS, I ATTENDED A CELEBRATION HELD BY THE DESPOT OF KANDAHAR."

I SMELL A PARTY, BONEBAG!

"THE DESPOT SEEMED FASCINATED BY ME..."

"WE HAD A NICE CHAT ABOUT HIS HOBBY..."

"IT TURNED OUT HE WAS A COLLECTING NUT...MATHEMATICAL EPHEMERA, PYTHAGORAS' COMPASSES, NEWTON'S APPLE, GORON'S PHOTON-COUNTER, THAT SORT OF THING. I SOON ASCERTAINED WHAT OBJECT HE COVETED ABOVE ALL OTHERS..."

...A PERFECT MATHEMATICAL MODEL OF THE UNIVERSE FORMED OUT OF ROCK CRYSTAL, REVERED BY SOME PRIMITIVES IN A CITY WHICH ALL RECORDS SHOWED WAS DOOMED TO EXTINCTION BY AN EARTHQUAKE...

...AND YOU'D PAY FOR THAT, WOULD YOU?

"IT WAS ON EARTH, CAPTAIN. *YOUR* EARTH. PERHAPS I WAS RASH, BUT I **WAS** A LITTLE *UNDER THE WEATHER!*"

"MY PLAN WAS FOR THE LIZARD TO ESTABLISH THE EXACT LOCATION OF THE MODEL, AND THEN FOR FASCINATION TO REACH IN AND REMOVE IT... FROM THE JAWS OF THE EARTHQUAKE AS IT WERE..."

"...IN THIS WAY, SINCE THE MODEL WAS DOOMED TO DESTRUCTION, REMOVING IT WOULD NOT INTERRUPT ANY CAUSAL CONTINUUM."

"UNFORTUNATELY, THOUGH DEAR FASCINATION IS A LOYAL CREATURE, HER INTELLIGENCE IS BARELY EQUAL TO ONE OF YOUR DOMESTIC PETS..."

"AFTER NUMEROUS ATTEMPTS, RESULTING IN THE APPROPRIATION OF ASSORTED TRINKETS, WE REALISED THAT SHE COULD NOT IDENTIFY THE MODEL WITHOUT ITS SCENT."

"WHICH, INCIDENTALLY, IS HOW SHE LOCATED YOU SO EASILY."

"I DECIDED TO TRY THE 'GODS-FROM-THE-SKY' APPROACH."

ON YOUR KNEES, INKLE DOGS!

Inca, Mother. Call them Incas.

"...USUALLY VERY EFFECTIVE, IF APPLIED WITH SUBTLETY."

"THEY SHOWED DUE DEFERENCE..."

There's certainly a lot of gold about.

HOW VULGAR.

"...AND THE RIGHT AMOUNT OF FEAR."

"EVEN THE PRIESTHOOD WAS SMILING AND OBSEQUIOUS..."

"THEY OFFERED TRIBUTE..."

"WE ASKED FOR THE CRYSTAL MODEL."

"THEY SAID THE BANQUET WAS A NECESSARY PART OF THE ACCEPTANCE CEREMONY. IT PAINS ME THAT I DID NOT SUSPECT..."

GRUUUMBL

"THE FIRST TREMORS STRUCK AT THE SAME TIME AS THE POISON IN THE FRUIT."

"FORTUNATELY, FASCINATION'S SPECIES FEEDS ON THE EXCESS EMOTIONAL ENERGY OF SENTIENT BEINGS, SO SHE HAD 'NOT EATEN ANY OF THE FRUIT.'"

Motherrrr...

FLUUB!

"I ONLY JUST MANAGED TO TELEPATHICALLY INSTRUCT HER TO BRING YOU HERE BEFORE I PASSED GRACEFULLY INTO UNCONSCIOUSNESS."

"WE CAME TO DOWN HERE WITH THAT CACKLING HIGH PRIEST GLOATING OVER US..."

...SO, GODS, IF YOU REMAIN IN THE COOL WATER, THE MANY PARASITE EGGS WHICH YOU HAVE EATEN MAY NOT HATCH!

"I WAS HUMILIATED."

ENOUGH, ENOUGH! YOU'LL HAVE ME IN TEARS! BASICALLY, WHAT YOU'RE SAYING IS THAT, THROUGH ARROGANCE AND INEPTITUDE, YOU'VE BLUNDERED INTO DISASTER AND TURNED ALL YOUR FRIENDS AGAINST YOU. YES?

Not me, Mother.

WHAT DO YOU EXPECT ME TO DO?

YOU COULD SHOW SYMPATHY, CAPTAIN. IF NOT FOR ME, THEN FOR MY COMPANION...

YOU FAT HYPOCRITE!

YOU COULD ALSO FETCH THE REMEDY...

THE LIZARD GOT THE SECRET FROM THE HIGH PRIEST'S MIND. THE RAW MATERIALS ARE, AS ONE WOULD SUSPECT, BOTH RARE AND INACCESSIBLE.

THIS MAKES US EVEN... RIGHT?

HURRY, BRIAN, I CAN FEEL THE EARTHQUAKE BUILDING...

161

HE FINDS IT. A MYSTIC HERB GROWING IN THE RUINS OF A TEMPLE GARDEN, HIGH ON THE SLOPES OF A DISTANT MOUNTAIN.

...AND, IN THE SILENCE OF THE FILTERED LIGHT, TUGS IT FROM THE SHELTERING EARTH.

AS IT SQUIRMS AND WRIGGLES IN HIS HAND, A THIN HIGH WHISTLE DRILLS THE AIR.

WINGS BEAT AND TALONS GLEAM. A HUGE SHADOW RIDES THE HUMMING AIR.

INSTINCT TWISTS HIM FROM THE CUTTING CLAWS.

BIRDS!

CREEEECH!

BUT SURELY NO BIRD AS BIG AS THIS EVER LIVED ON EARTH.

I'VE NEVER SEEN AN ARCHAEOLOGICAL SPECIMEN OF ANY-THING LIKE THIS ... THEY MUST BE MUTATIONS OF SOME SORT!

AWK!

NO TIME TO WORRY ABOUT THAT NOW...

CRAAW!

THE EARTHQUAKES ARE INTENSIFYING. I'D BETTER MOVE...

ALL THAT DRESSING UP, THE PARASITE EGGS, THE GIANT BIRDS, ALL WASTED...

I-I HAD NOT FORSEEN ANY POSSIBILITY OF THIS CAPTAIN BRITAIN'S INVOLVEMENT...

IT JUST WAS NOT LOGICAL. MY IMPERSONATION OF THE DESPOT OF KANDAHAR WAS BRILLIANT! GATECRASHER WAS COMPLETELY FOOLED!

AND YAP NEVER SUSPECTED THAT I WAS THE PRIMITIVES' HIGH PRIEST, EVEN WHEN I ALLOWED HIM TO PICK THE LOCATION OF THE ROOT FROM MY MIND. MY PSI SCREEN WAS IMPECCABLE.

MY PLAN WAS PERFECT! GATECRASHER SHOULD HAVE SENT FASCINATION FOR THE ROOT AND THE CITY WOULD HAVE BEEN DESTROYED BY THE TIME SHE HAD SUBDUED THE BIRDS. THEN SHE WOULD HAVE JOINED **US**.

IT WAS NOT MEANT TO BE. YOU CANNOT ALTER HISTORY...

YES, YES, I KNOW. FASCINATION WON'T JOIN THE SQUAD FOR ANOTHER THREE CENTURIES, BY WHICH TIME I'LL BE LONG DEAD AND REPLACED BY A HAIRY CYBORG.

BUT IT WOULD HAVE MADE THE FUTURE EASIER TO ACCEPT IF IT DIDN'T INCLUDE GATECRASHER. SHE'S GOING TO GIVE US A LOT OF TROUBLE!

Mother, I'm scared. It won't be long now. The main tremor pattern is building...

HEY! WHERE ARE YOU GOING?

I'LL BE BACK...

MEG..?

...IN A MINUTE.

BY THE MILLION TEATS OF BLESHU, **BRING ME THAT PLANT!** WE ONLY HAVE SECONDS!

LEAVE US, CAPTAIN. I...I WOULD LIKE TO MAINTAIN SOME DIGNITY... **ACH!** AND THE EFFECTS OF THIS CURE... **UNGH!** ARE GOING TO BE SOMEWHAT DRASTIC...

It hurts, Mother. It hurts!

GRUUMMBL

OUTSIDE HE SHIVERS WITH UNEASE AS HE BREATHES THE LAST MOMENTS OF A DOOMED CIVILISATION.

WHERE HAVE YOU BEEN?

OH, JUST HAVING A LOOK AROUND.

AWESOME, ISN'T IT? I WONDER IF THIS COULD BE ONE OF THE LEGENDARY LOST CITIES...LIKE EL DORADO?

KREEEKUMBLE

C'MON, CHILD. IT'S NOW OR NEVER! WE EITHER GET CRUSHED FROM THE OUTSIDE, OR EATEN FROM WITHIN! **LET'S GO!**

You— you called me child...

QUIET, LIZARD, JUST CONCENTRATE.. FIND THE FIX AND...

165

"...WHERE WE WANT TO GO."

OH, NO. NOT *HERE*.

C'MON, MEGGAN, LET'S GET OUT OF HERE. BRADDOCK MANOR ISN'T MY HOME ANY MORE. WE'LL HAVE TO...

BRIAN! LOOK!

CAPTAIN BRITAINS—*TWO* OF THEM!

IT'S LINDA... AND BETSY!

BETSY... WHY? HOW COULD SHE...?

IT WASN'T ENOUGH TO JUST HELP THE R.C.X. TAKE OVER THE MANOR. NO, NOW SHE'S TURNED AGAINST ME, JOINED THEM, FORCED ME OUT...

...WELL, IF SHE THINKS SHE CAN REPLACE ME, LET HER TRY...

I QUIT.

KRUNCH

Next: It's Hard To Be A Hero

166

AS A FRINGE GROUP WE'RE NOT VERY POPULAR IN CERTAIN INFLUENTIAL CIRCLES—BUT OUR ASSOCIATION WITH A NATIONAL HERO WOULD ENSURE FAVOUR WITH THE P.M.

WITHOUT THE PROTECTION THAT WOULD AFFORD, ALL WE'VE DONE SO FAR—INCLUDING THE SAFETY OF THE WARPIES—WILL BE IN JEOPARDY.

WE NEED **YOU**, BETSY. **YOU** SHARE THE **POWER**.

WHY CAN'T **YOU** DO IT, LINDA? YOU DID IT ON YOUR OWN EARTH...

BUT MAYBE I COULD BE YOUR PARTNER FOR A FEW MONTHS, AND GIVE YOU THE BENEFIT OF MY EXPERIENCE...

AND WITH A BIT OF LUCK, BRIAN MAY HAVE SEEN SENSE AND COME HOME BY THEN...

I'VE ADAPTED THIS UNIFORM TO MATCH YOUR INDIVIDUAL PSI-RHYTHMS, AND FASHIONED IT IN A MANNER THAT SHOULD SATISFY YOUR SENSE OF STYLE.

NO.

I'M SORRY, BETSY, I'D NEVER INTENDED MY INVOLVEMENT TO BE MORE THAN SHORT-TERM.

I HAVE MY OWN LIFE NOW, AND I'D LIKE TO GET BACK TO IT...

OKAY, **OKAY!** I'LL... GIVE IT A GO...

ANY CHANCE YOU COULD DO SOMETHING WITH MINE, JEEVES? THE HOOD PUSHES THESE BEADS INTO MY SKULL, AND...

NO, I WON'T WEAR IT...

IT BELONGED TO THAT... THAT, IMPOSTER.

SO? HE'S DEAD MEAT NOW. **YOU** KILLED HIM—PRETTY CONVINCINGLY BY ALL ACCOUNTS. THE SUIT'S **SPOILS OF WAR.** YOU WON IT, FAIR AND SQUARE.

HAS ANYONE EVER TOLD YOU YOU'RE REALLY **SICK**, MICHAEL!

YEAH, ALL THE TIME, BUT AT LEAST I'M NOT AFRAID OF WEARING DEAD MEN'S CLOTHES.

169

...AND OF THEIR KILLER.

SLAYMASTER!

BE CALM, AND YOUR DEATH WILL BE SWIFT AND PAINLESS.

...I'M GOING TO ENJOY IT!

NEVER! I'M NOT JUST A TELEPATH NOW, I HAVE POWER, REAL POWER. AND FOR ONCE I'M NOT GOING TO BE AFRAID TO USE IT...

YOUR POWERS ARE INDEED IMPRESSIVE, WOMAN. BUT I ALSO POSSESS AN AMPLIFIER COSTUME, CREATED BY THE VIXEN'S TECHNICIANS TO ENHANCE MY OWN UNIQUE ABILITIES.

WELL STOP MESSING ABOUT, SLAYMASTER, AND USE IT!

QUIET, HAG, YOU'RE NEXT!

HAG? NOBODY CALLS THE VIXEN A HAG! KILL HER! CRUSH HER! RIP HER APART!

OUF!

YOU SHALL REGRET YOUR FOLLY, WOMAN. NOW YOU WILL SUFFER. AND FEEL PAIN.

WUD

MUCH PAIN!

REALITY CAN NO LONGER BE IGNORED...

AEEEE

...IT IS CRUEL, AND BRUTAL, AND BLIND.

171

OTHER REALITIES CAN BE BEAUTIFUL.

MEGGAN, YOU LITTLE...

LAST ONE HOME MAKES LUNCH!

HOME, A TOWER OF SOLITUDE AND TRANQUILITY BOUGHT WITH INCA GOLD.

OH, BRIAN, YOU CHEAT!

I'M STILL NOT USED TO HOW WELL YOU CAN FLY WITHOUT YOUR COSTUME.

AND I'D NEVER HAVE KNOWN I COULD, IF I HADN'T PUT IT IN MOTHBALLS — WHAT IS IT — ALMOST FIVE MONTHS AGO NOW.

YES, IT'S DIFFICULT TO KEEP TRACK OF TIME HERE. IT'S SO PEACEFUL.

I'M STARTING TO THINK THAT THE UNIFORM WASN'T SO MUCH AN AMPLIFIER, AS A CRUTCH THAT STOPPED ME FROM DEVELOPING MY FULL ABILITIES AND...

BRIAN?

AND...

BETSY!

AIEEEEE

BETSY NEEDS ME... YOU STAY HERE.

BUT...

STAY HERE!

...I WANT TO BE WITH YOU...

HE DOESN'T HEAR. HE IS A DOT IN THE SOUTHERN SKY.

NOW, WOMAN, BEFORE I RELEASE YOU FROM YOUR MISERY, TELL ME WHERE THE *ORIGINAL* CAPTAIN BRITAIN IS. I HAVE A DEBT TO REPAY. HE TRICKED ME WHEN LAST WE MET...

GIVE IT A REST, DEARIE. YOU DON'T WANT TO TALK HER TO DEATH...

C'MON, DUCKIE, MAKE IT EASY ON YOURSELF...

GO T'HELL, Y'OLD *HAG*!

FOOL!

WHUP!

HURT HER! MAKE HER SQUEAL, MAKE HER *BEG* TO DIE!

WHAT..?

UH?

KABOOM!

Brian..?

OH, BETSY... NO!

AH! THE REAL CAPTAIN BRITAIN AT LAST! I RECOGNISE THE LUMBERING HULK... IN TRUTH IT COULD BE NONE OTHER.

WHY HAVE YOU DONE THIS?

SHE WAS NOT A WORTHY FOE, SHE DESERVED NO BETTER.

AAAAANNIMAALL.!!

YOU DARE TO FACE ME WITHOUT YOUR AMPLIFIER COSTUME? HA!

174

RARRRG!

SKRNNNG

LET'S GET OUT OF HERE WHILE THERE'S STILL TIME, VINCENT— WE SEEM TO HAVE SUFFERED A SLIGHT SETBACK...

...AND WE HAVE A LORRY LOAD OF HOSTAGES TO DISPOSE OF.

FOOL! YOU HAVE NOT THE STRENGTH TO KILL...

BRADDOCK MANOR...

SHBLAMM!

YOU GUTLESS WONDERS! YOU SENT BETSY OUT TO DIE WHILE YOU HID HERE!

WE HAD NO CHOICE, IT...

NO CHOICE!? BETSY'S BEEN BLINDED AND BEATEN HALF TO DEATH!

DON'T YOU DARE TRY TO JUSTIFY THAT! JUST GET OUT, OR I'LL DO SOMETHING YOU'LL REGRET.

JEEVES, PLEASE DO WHAT YOU CAN...

YES, CAPTAIN.

LET ME HELP...

DON'T TOUCH HER! I TOLD YOU TO LEAVE, NOW!

NO, BRIAN. NO—I WANT HIM TO STAY.

Captain BRITAIN

Should Auld Acquaintance...

DECEMBER 24TH. 11·30 P.M.

THIS IS HOW CHRISTMAS SHOULD BE...

SCRIPT AND PENCILS: ALAN DAVIS
INKS : MARK FARMER
LETTERS : ANNIE HALFACREE
EDITOR : IAN RIMMER

...CUDDLED UP IN FRONT OF A LOG FIRE WITH MINCE PIES, BRANDY AND NO INTERRUPTIONS.

KNOK NOK

I REALLY WISH YOU HADN'T SAID THAT...

WHO CAN IT BE? IT'S FAR TOO LATE FOR A SOCIAL CALL...

WELL, UNLESS SANTA IS HAVING PROBLEMS FINDING THE CHIMNEY, IT COULD WELL BE MORE...

TROUBLE.

DAI THOMAS!

I'M FLATTERED THAT YOU SHOULD REMEMBER ME, CAPTAIN, IT'S BEEN A LONG TIME...

DON'T BOTHER DENYING THAT YOU ARE CAPTAIN BRITAIN. I FIGURED IT OUT SOME TIME AGO, AND I'VE KEPT TRACK OF YOU EVER SINCE.

ROUTINE POLICE WORK, REALLY. BUT THEN I SUPPOSE YOU THINK ALL POLICE-MEN ARE STUPID.

NO, JUST YOU.

DON'T PUSH IT, BRADDOCK! I DON'T HAVE YOUR PEDIGREE BUT I'M MORE THAN A BOYO FROM THE VALLEY WITH NOTHING BUT COAL DUST BETWEEN MY EARS! I...

178

I...I'M SORRY.

IT WAS VERY DIFFICULT FOR ME TO HAVE COME HERE. I'VE HAD TO SWALLOW MY PRIDE...

AND A FAIR AMOUNT OF DUTCH COURAGE.

I'LL — I'LL GET TO THE POINT.

THERE HAVE BEEN A SERIES OF EXCEPTIONALLY BRUTAL AND INEXPLICABLE MURDERS UP IN GLASGOW.

HOW DOES THAT CONCERN ME?

ALL TWENTY-SEVEN VICTIMS WERE KNOWN VILLAINS, SO IT'S LOGICAL TO SUSPECT SOME SORT OF GANG-WAR.

I WANT YOU TO POSE AS THE EMISSARY OF A CRIME SYNDICATE MOVING INTO THE GLASGOW AREA. HOPEFULLY, WHOEVER IS BEHIND THE MURDERS WILL FEEL THREATENED ENOUGH TO COME AFTER YOU.

BUT WHY DO YOU NEED ME? SURELY CATCHING MURDERERS IS "ROUTINE POLICE WORK!"

THIS IS NO ORDINARY MURDERER! ALL THE VICTIMS HAVE BEEN HORRENDOUSLY MUTILATED... AND AT INCREDIBLE SPEED!

ONE WAS ALONE FOR LESS THAN A MINUTE, YET HE WAS VIRTUALLY DISMANTLED. A BUTCHER WITH A CHAINSAW COULDN'T INFLICT AS MUCH DAMAGE SO QUICKLY.

ANOTHER VICTIM WAS CARRYING A NINE MILLIMETER UZI. HE FIRED A BURST OF APPROXIMATELY TWENTY ROUNDS AT HIS ATTACKER. EIGHTEEN BULLETS WERE RECOVERED — ELEVEN WERE SLICED OR SHREDDED, FOUR WERE FLATTENED, AND THREE WERE FUSED INTO A SPHERE.

NOW I'VE LOST THREE MEN — REAL PRO'S WHO WOULDN'T HAVE TAKEN ANY UNNECESSARY RISKS. ALL WERE MUTILATED BEFORE THEY COULD RADIO FOR ASSISTANCE...

AFTER THIRTY YEARS ON THE FORCE I THOUGHT I'D SEEN EVERYTHING - BUT I CAN'T BEGIN TO IMAGINE WHAT SORT OF EVIL MONSTROSITY IS BEHIND THIS...

I'M SCARED, BRADDOCK, AND I'VE NOWHERE ELSE TO TURN. PLEASE, YOU'VE GOT TO HELP ME...

DARKMOOR.

UH!

ROMA!

I'M SORRY—I FELL ASLEEP WHILE I WAS WAITING. I CAME EARLY. IT ISN'T EVERYDAY I GET A SUMMONS FROM THE GUARDIAN OF THE MULTIVERSE...

YOU DREAMT OF YOUR HUSBAND.

NOT A DREAM...A NIGHTMARE.

RICK SENT ME HERE WHEN MY EARTH WAS BEING DESTROYED.

I WATCHED THE FURY KILL HIM...

IT IS AS A RESULT OF YOUR HUSBAND'S ACTIONS THAT I HAVE BEEN FORCED TO SUMMON YOU.

YOU ARE NOT OF THIS WORLD. YOUR PRESENCE IS AN ANOMALY THAT HAS PREVENTED THIS CONTINUUM FROM HEALING THE WOUNDS INFLICTED BY THE JASPERS CREATURE...

THE DEFORMED CHILDREN YOU CALL WARPIES CONTINUE TO BE BORN.

THE CRAZY GANG'S INSANITY SURVIVES TO POLLUTE THE INNOCENCE OF THIS LAND, WHEN IT SHOULD HAVE PERISHED WITH ITS CREATOR.

YOU CANNOT REMAIN, OR THE DECAY WILL PERSIST.

WE MUST LEAVE FOR OTHERWORLD IMMEDIATELY.

180

DECEMBER 25TH. 7·30 A.M.

I DON'T LIKE SNORING SEE, SO I'M GONNA WASTE YA! GET UP, PIG, AN TAKE IT LIKE A MAN!

WASSAMMATU...

BRADDOCK! WHAT THE DEVIL ARE YOU PLAYING AT?

SORRY, BRIAN, THAT WON'T SCARE A GLASGOW GODFATHER. IT SOUNDS TOO CORNY. CAN'T YOU TRY TO SOUND A BIT MORE LIKE CLINT EASTWOOD?

THIS ISN'T A GAME! IT'S A DANGEROUS BUSINESS...

CLINT WHO?

HEY, MAYBE I SHOULD DO THE TALKING, BRIAN. PLAY IT HARD AND BITCHY. YOU KNOW, LIKE JOAN COLLINS!

MEGGAN, YOU ARE LIVING PROOF THAT TELEVISION CAUSES IRREPARABLE BRAIN DAMAGE!

CAN'T YOU TWO BE SERIOUS!?

HOW SHOULD I WEAR MY HAIR?

WHAT DO YOU THINK, MR. THOMAS? LONG AND BLONDE?

SHORT AND DARK?

I KNOW, BUSHY AND AUBURN.

NOW I NEED THE RIGHT CLOTHES, AND YOU'LL NEED SOMETHING MORE MACHO, BRIAN.

HOW—HOW DID SHE DO THAT, BRADDOCK?

TO BE HONEST, I'M NOT SURE. MEGGAN'S POWERS ARE STILL DEVELOPING, BUT AMONG HER MANY BUDDING ABILITIES IS THE CAPACITY TO MANIPULATE HER FORM...

I THOUGHT YOU WOULD HAVE KNOWN ALL ABOUT THAT, AS THE LEADER OF THE CAMPAIGN AGAINST SUPERHUMANS!

181

BRADDOCK MANOR.

ELIZABETH HAS MADE A REMARKABLE RECOVERY, GABRIEL.

YES, ALISON. THOUGH IT'S DUE MORE TO HER SPIRIT THAN JEEVES. RECENTLY HE SEEMS TO BE ENTIRELY DEVOTED TO EMMA...

RUN ALONG AND WATCH THE CHILDREN OPENING THEIR PRESENTS, EMMA. I HAVE ALL THE PREPARATIONS IN HAND.

THANK YOU, JEEVES! YOU'RE SO CONSIDERATE!

WHY DO YOU TOLERATE HER? SHE'S A WASTE OF SPACE... SHE SPENDS MOST OF HER TIME ASLEEP, ANYWAY.

YES, MICHAEL, THAT IS WHAT ALERTED ME TO HER CONDITION.

CONDITION?

PRIOR TO THE CAPTAIN'S RETURN IN NINETEEN EIGHTY-TWO, I MALFUNCTIONED FOR A PERIOD OF SEVEN YEARS.

DURING THAT TIME I TOOK CONTROL OF EMMA'S MIND AND HELD HER IN THRALL. THE EXPERIENCE CAUSED A GREAT DEAL OF DAMAGE TO HER NERVOUS SYSTEM. HER CONDITION IS DETERIORATING...

I HAVE EXHAUSTED ALL OF MY RESOURCES IN AN ATTEMPT TO FIND A CURE, BUT THERE IS NOTHING I CAN DO TO SAVE HER. SHE WILL DIE WITHIN THE NEXT YEAR.

STEADY ON, JEEVES! YOU'RE A COMPUTER-GENERATED SOLID LIGHT HOLOGRAM—YOU SOUND LIKE A LOVE SICK MORTAL!

BUILDABLOX

182

BRADDOCK MANOR.

THANKS BUT NO THANKS, GABRIEL. I'D RATHER BE SIGHTLESS THAN HAVE YOU FIT THOSE BALL BEARINGS TO MY HEAD.

PHOTO-RECEPTIVE CYBERNETIC IMPLANTATIONS ARE BETTER THAN BEING BLIND, ELIZABETH.

I'M NOT BLIND. MY PSYCHIC POWERS MORE THAN COMPENSATE FOR MY LACK OF SIGHT. IT'S LIKE BEING ABLE TO... SMELL COLOUR... TO TASTE FORM... AND HEAR DISTANCE.

IT MAKES ME FEEL SORRY FOR PEOPLE THAT ARE RESTRICTED TO VISION.

YES, SWITZERLAND IS BEAUTIFUL, AND ALISON'S CHÂTEAU IS STRAIGHT OUT OF A FAIRYTALE. IT'S THE IDEAL PLACE FOR A HOLIDAY...

ALL I WANT NOW IS TO BE WITH YOU, AND TO LEAVE THE MANOR. IT ISN'T MY HOME ANY MORE.

I'M LOOKING FORWARD TO THE CHANGE OF SCENERY...

...OR A HONEYMOON...?

MICHAEL, I WANTED YOU TO BE THE FIRST TO SEE THIS SYNTHETIC FORM I HAVE CREATED TO ACCOMPANY EMMA ON A LITTLE CRUISE I HAVE PLANNED FOR HER.

YOU'RE LEAVING?

NO, BUT I CANNOT PROJECT HOLOGRAMS BEYOND THE MANOR'S OUTER BOUNDARY, AND IT WILL ALLOW ME TO DISPOSE OF THIS SOLID LIGHT FACADE, WHICH I CREATED SOLELY FOR EMMA'S BENEFIT.

MY LADY ROMA HAS INFORMED ME THAT THE CAUSE OF THE WARPIES HAS BEEN REMOVED, AND NO MORE WILL BE BORN...

...I AM INSTRUCTED TO PROTECT AND PREPARE THOSE THAT ALREADY EXIST FOR THE CHALLENGE OF THEIR FUTURE.

YOU AND THE RCX MAY REMAIN TO ASSIST ME IN MY TASK, BUT PLEASE BE ADVISED...

I AM IN CONTROL OF THIS SITUATION.

GLASGOW. DECEMBER 30TH. 6:30 P.M.

REDONDO'S ABATTOIR

I'VE LET THE LOCAL GRAPEVINE KNOW THAT WE'RE STAYING OUT HERE TO RECEIVE A CONSIGNMENT OF HEROIN.

I WANT ANY CONFRONTATION WITH THIS SUPER-ASSASSIN OUT HERE, BRADDOCK, AWAY FROM INNOCENT BYSTANDERS.

YOU CAN'T BE SERIOUS, THOMAS! WHAT'S WRONG WITH THE HOTEL?

7:15 P.M.

WE'VE WALKED SO FAR THESE PAST FEW DAYS MY FEET ARE ACHING!

AREN'T YOU USED TO HIGH HEELS?

I'M NOT USED TO WALKING! BEING ABLE TO FLY, WE ONLY WALK TO APPEAR NORMAL IN PUBLIC.

10:35 P.M.

SO WHY IS A CHIEF INSPECTOR OF SCOTLAND YARD OPERATING IN GLASGOW?

THE OLD SCHOOL TIE DISAPPROVED OF MY "ABRASIVE ATTITUDE". I WAS PUTTING TOO MANY NOSES OUT OF JOINT. I WAS PROMOTED TO A NEWLY FORMED NATIONAL INVESTIGATION UNIT...

YOU KNOW WHAT THEY SAY— UPWARDS AND OUTWARDS...

00:05 A.M.

IT SICKENS ME THAT ORGANISATIONS LIKE THE RCX ARE ALLOWED TO OPERATE IN THIS COUNTRY. THEY'RE **CORRUPT**. THEY **PERVERT** THE LAW.

I KNOW ALL ABOUT THE RCX. THEY WORMED THEIR WAY INTO MY HOME, TOOK IT OVER, AND DROVE ME OUT. THEN THEY TURNED MY SISTER AGAINST ME, AND VERY NEARLY KILLED HER...

THAT'S WHY MEGGAN AND I MOVED TO THE LIGHTHOUSE...

1:45 A.M.

THE PRESS MADE MY CAMPAIGN AGAINST SUPERHUMANS SOUND UNREASONABLE, BRIAN. THEY MADE ME SOUND LIKE A FOOL BECAUSE I PROTESTED WHEN MY WIFE WAS MURDERED BY THE CARELESS STUPIDITY OF BRAWLING "SUPER HEROES"...

I KNOW HOW EASILY IT CAN HAPPEN. BUT I DIDN'T ASK FOR THE POWER, OR THE RESPONSIBILITY...

THE ONLY DIFFERENCE BETWEEN US IS THAT MY MISTAKES ARE IN PROPORTION TO MY POWERS, AND —IF I'M LUCKY— SO ARE MY SUCCESSES.

4:30 A.M.

LOOK, YOU'VE SMASHED UP THE PREMISES OF EVERY LOCAL OUTFIT — THEY'RE BOUND TO WANT REVENGE. IT'S ONLY A MATTER OF TIME TILL THE EXECUTIONER TURNS UP.

IN FACT, THE GRAPEVINE HAS ALREADY CONFIRMED OUR IMPENDING DEATHS. THEY CALL THE ASSASSIN **SHOULDERS McGILL.**

I HOPE HE'S NOT AS BIG AS HE SOUNDS!

THE TYRANT, MASTREX OPUL LUN SAT-YR-NIN IS MASSACRING HER OWN PEOPLE...

BRIAN TOLD ME ABOUT HER. SHE RULES THE EARTH OF **KAPTAIN BRITON**—THE DOPPLEGANGER OF BRIAN THAT BETSY KILLED.

TO SHOW MY GRATITUDE, I HAVE A GIFT. PLEASE THINK OF YOUR HUSBAND. OF YOUR LAST MOMENTS TOGETHER...

I DON'T...

PLEASE.

INDEED, A WORLD THAT DESPERATELY NEEDS A CAPTAIN. AND SINCE YOU ARE A CAPTAIN WITHOUT A WORLD, THERE IS AN OBVIOUS SOLUTION...

WELL, I HAVEN'T ANY OTHER PRESSING ENGAGEMENTS... I MIGHT AS WELL GIVE IT A GO!

"THE FURY WAS SLAUGHTERING MY WORLD'S HEROES..."

"HE WAS UNSTOPPABLE."

"WE WERE TERRIFIED..."

"RICK SAID THE TELEPORTER WAS OUR ONLY CHANCE."

"THE FURY CAME AFTER US..."

"IT LUNGED AT RICK..."

"BUT HE DISAPPEARED."

"FOR A MOMENT THE FURY WAS CONFUSED, BUT HE IGNORED HIS LOSS AND CONTINUED THE SLAUGHTER."

...I DON'T UNDERSTAND! I REMEMBER IT HAPPENING LIKE THAT... BUT IT DIDN'T...

RICK

IT DID. BECAUSE I REACHED BACK IN TIME, TO THE INSTANT BEFORE HIS DEATH, AND BROUGHT HIM HERE.

DECEMBER 31ST. 11.55 P.M.

COME ON — YOU CAN'T DOSS HERE, YOU'LL HAVE TO MOVE ON.

A DON'T DOSS, AN' A GO WHERE A WANT. ANYWAY, A HAVE BUSINESS HERE.

WHAT BUSINESS?

A MESSAGE FOR THE TART AN' THE BIG MAN...

TELL ME — I'LL PASS IT ON.

IF YER WITH THEM, THE MESSAGE IS FOR YER AS WELL. THE LORD BLESSED ME WI' A CHILD. AN ANGEL. MY ANGEL OF DEATH. SILVER DEATH. GLITTERING SCYTHES OF SWEET RELEASE...

IT IS HIS MISSION. HE CHOSE ME, AN' GAVE ME BROAD SHOULDERS T'CARRY THE BURDEN...

AN' CARRY IT WI' PRIDE. SHOULDERS McGILL IS PROUD T' DO THE LORD'S WORK!

TIME SLOWS FOR DAI THOMAS. HE HAS GROWN CARELESS IN THE PROTECTION OF THE CAPTAIN. HE HAD FELT SECURE...

BUT NOW HE IS ALONE.

KRNNG

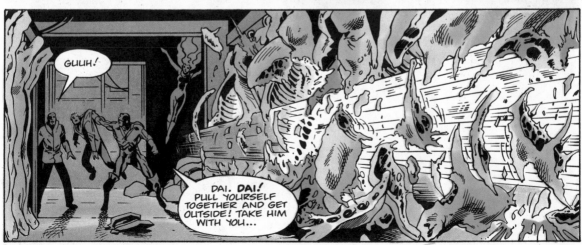

GUUH!

DAI. DAI! PULL YOURSELF TOGETHER AND GET OUTSIDE! TAKE HIM WITH YOU...

NEVER THE END.

BAD MOON RISING

Plot and Art:
ALAN DAVIS
Script and Letters:
STEVE CRADDOCK
Colour:
STEVE WHITE
Editor:
CHRIS GILL
Originally presented in
**THE MIGHTY WORLD
OF MARVEL** No. 14
July 1984

TEA AND SYMPATHY

Script and Art:
ALAN DAVIS
Letters:
STEVE CRADDOCK
Colour:
STEVE WHITE
Editor:
CHRIS GILL
Originally presented in
**THE MIGHTY WORLD
OF MARVEL** No. 15
August 1984

IN ALL THE OLD FAMILIAR PLACES

Plot and Art:
ALAN DAVIS
Script:
MIKE COLLINS
Letters:
STEVE CRADDOCK
Colour:
STEVE WHITE
Editor:
CHRIS GILL
Originally presented in
**THE MIGHTY WORLD
OF MARVEL** No. 16
September 1984

PICTURES, PUZZLES & PAWNS

Title Design:
JOHN TOMLINSON

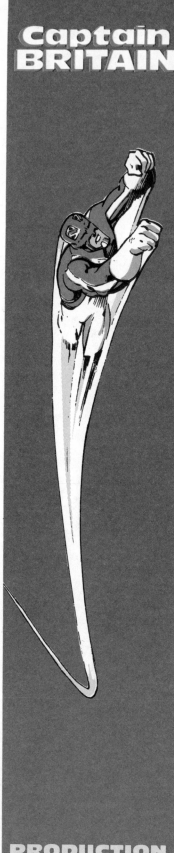

Captain BRITAIN

PRODUCTION CREDITS

191

Colour:
STEVE WHITE
Editor:
CHRIS GILL
Originally presented as
MYTH, MEMORY AND LEGEND,
in **CAPTAIN BRITAIN** No. 1
January 1985

LAW AND DISORDER

Colour:
STUART PLACE
Originally presented in
CAPTAIN BRITAIN No. 2
February 1985

FLOTSAM AND JETSAM

Colour:
STUART PLACE
Originally presented in
CAPTAIN BRITAIN No. 3
March 1985

SID'S STORY

Title Lettering:
ALAN DAVIS
Colour:
STUART PLACE
Originally presented in
CAPTAIN BRITAIN No. 4
April 1985

DOUBLE GAME

Title Design:
RICHARD STARKINGS
Colour:
STUART PLACE
Originally presented in
CAPTAIN BRITAIN No. 5
May 1985

A LONG WAY FROM HOME

Title Lettering:
RICHARD STARKINGS
Colour:
STUART PLACE
Originally presented in
CAPTAIN BRITAIN No. 6
June 1985

Captain BRITAIN

THINGS FALL APART

Title Lettering:
RICHARD STARKINGS
Colour:
STUART PLACE
Originally presented in
CAPTAIN BRITAIN No. 7
July 1985

CHILDHOOD'S END

Title Lettering:
ALAN DAVIS
Colour:
LOUISE CASSELL
Originally presented in
CAPTAIN BRITAIN No. 8
August 1985

WINDS OF CHANGE

Title Lettering:
ALAN DAVIS
Colour:
LOUISE CASSELL
Originally presented in
CAPTAIN BRITAIN No. 9
September 1985

AFRICAN NIGHTMARE

Title Lettering:
ALAN DAVIS
Colour:
STUART PLACE
Originally presented in
CAPTAIN BRITAIN No. 10
October 1985

THE HOUSE OF BABA YAGA

Title Lettering:
RICHARD STARKINGS
Colour:
NICK ABADZIS
Originally presented in
CAPTAIN BRITAIN No. 11
November 1985

ALARMS AND EXCURSIONS

Title Lettering:
RICHARD STARKINGS
Colour:
STUART PLACE
Originally presented in
CAPTAIN BRITAIN No. 12
December 1985

IT'S HARD TO BE A HERO

Title Lettering:
RICHARD STARKINGS
Colour:
STUART PLACE
Originally presented in
CAPTAIN BRITAIN No. 13
January 1986

SHOULD AULD ACQUAINTANCE

Title Lettering:
ALAN DAVIS
Colour:
STEVE WHITE
Originally presented in
CAPTAIN BRITAIN No. 14
February 1986

Original Series
Assistant Editor:
SIMON FURMAN

Trade Paperback
Editor and Designer:
RICHARD STARKINGS

Trade Paperback
Assistant Editors:
**ANDREW SEDDON
PERI GODBOLD**

Managing Editor:
JENNY O'CONNOR

Production:
**ALISON KINGWILL
JEZ METEYARD**

PRODUCTION CREDITS

OUTRODUCTION

I f it's hard to be a hero . . . it's harder still to find a hero a home. As comic strip characters go, Captain Britain went – all over the place. He first saw print in 1976, in his own title – **CAPTAIN BRITAIN** weekly, published by Marvel UK even though the strip was being originated by Marvel US. When his title folded, the Captain moved into the weekly SUPER SPIDER-MAN, then on to guest-star in the UK-originated BLACK KNIGHT strip in HULK COMIC, also a weekly.

In September 1981, Captain Britain and readers alike were introduced to artist Alan Davis, in the pages of the monthly MARVEL SUPERHEROES. In collaboration with editor Paul Neary and writer Dave Thorpe, Alan Davis redesigned not only the Captain's costume, but also his whole world.

Shortly after Alan Moore assumed the role of scriptwriter on the strip, the Captain moved on again, this time to the pages of THE DAREDEVILS, another monthly title – one destined to last only eleven issues. But still the good Captain wouldn't die and, after a brief stint in the monthly MIGHTY WORLD OF MARVEL he found himself in his own title again – **CAPTAIN BRITAIN**.

Guiding Brian Braddock along that checkered publishing path have been quite a few famous names, including John Buscema, John Byrne, Chris Claremont and, of course Alan Davis and Jamie Delano.

Let us not forget some of the 'smaller' names that have played a part in the Captain's life, however. Bernie Jaye was the editor of the strip during its brief stint in THE DAREDEVILS, Steve Craddock and Annie Halfacree provided painstaking lettering skills, and utterly indispensable to me, during my period at the helm, was one of the Captain's long-time assistants and friends, John Tomlinson.

Then there's me. By all means ask, ". . . and who are you?!" but believe me when I say that working on **CAPTAIN BRITAIN** provided me with my most pleasurable memories and experiences during my time in comics.

There's little more to add except . . . Cheers, Brian!

IAN RIMMER
Erstwhile Editor, **CAPTAIN BRITAIN**
New Malden, September 1988